Bits and pieces of the truth hit her with dynamic revelation.

Ashley's thoughts whirled like an off-center gyroscope. Too late she sensed a presence behind her.

Before she could move, a strong arm came around her and pinned her back in the chair. She glimpsed her attacker's face as a needle plunged into her neck.

"No...no...please, no!" Her cries echoed in her ears as her body disintegrated into a thousand floating pieces.

Brad's face came into her mind and the thought that she might never see him again made her cry out again.

And then her world went black.

LEONA KARR

CHARMED

TORONTO • NEW YORK • LONDON
AMSTERDAM • PARIS • SYDNEY • HAMBURG
STOCKHOLM • ATHENS • TOKYO • MILAN • MADRID
PRAGUE • WARSAW • BUDAPEST • AUCKLAND

In appreciation to Carol McNulty.
Many thanks for sharing such
wonderful background material.

ISBN-13: 978-0-373-22949-9
ISBN-10: 0-373-22949-6

CHARMED

This edition published by arrangement with Harlequin Books S.A.

www.eHarlequin.com

Printed in U.S.A.

ABOUT THE AUTHOR

A native of Colorado, Leona (Lee) Karr is the author of nearly forty books. Her favorite genres are romantic suspense and inspirational romance. Graduating from the University of Colorado with a B.A. and the University of Northern Colorado with an M.A., she taught as a reading specialist until her first book was published in 1980. She has been on the Waldenbooks bestseller list and nominated by *Romantic Times BOOKclub* as Best Romantic Saga and Best Gothic Author. She has been honored as the Rocky Mountain Fiction Writer of the Year, and received Colorado's Romance Writer of the Year award. Her books have been reprinted in more than a dozen foreign countries. She is a presenter at numerous writing conferences and has taught college courses in creative writing.

Books by Leona Karr

HARLEQUIN INTRIGUE

459—FOLLOW ME HOME
487—MYSTERY DAD
574—INNOCENT WITNESS
623—THE MYSTERIOUS TWIN
672—LOST IDENTITY
724—SEMIAUTOMATIC MARRIAGE
792—A DANGEROUS INHERITANCE
840—SHADOWS ON THE LAKE
900—STONEVIEW ESTATE
949—CHARMED

CAST OF CHARACTERS

Ashley Davis—She came to Greystone Island because her sister's life was in jeopardy. Did the same hidden menace wait in the foggy mists for her?

Brad Taylor—As sheriff on Greystone Island, he had to solve the mysteries of the past before he could bring a hidden murderer to justice.

Lorrie Davis—Ashley's sister's disappearance sparked a manhunt and reawakened the past.

Clayton Langdon—His wealth dominated his family and their island estate. What secrets haunted the Langdon mansion?

Jonathan Langdon—What was the oldest Langdon son's role in his family's web of violence and mystery?

Sloane—An island drifter. Was his obsession with Lorrie strong enough to hurt her and leave her for dead?

Dr. Hadley—As a close friend of the Langdons' and the island's only medical expert, what secrets did he have to hide?

Samantha Langdon—Did her guarded secrets set a lingering evil in motion?

Pamela Langdon—Was she the catalyst for all that happened?

Chapter One

Night shadows had already fallen when Ashley Davis's taxi reached the rugged coastline of Portland, Maine. Wisps of fog floated over choppy gray water, and a blanket of heavy, dark clouds heralded the approach of an Atlantic storm.

"You'll have to wait until morning for a ferry or hired boat," the driver briskly informed her as he opened the door and set down her single suitcase. "You won't be finding any transportation to Greystone Island this time of night."

"I have to," Ashley answered flatly as she handed him the fare.

As he drove off, Ashley slung the strap of her alligator purse over her shoulder and picked up her suitcase. Shivering in her lightweight beige knit jacket and slacks, she realized her San Francisco wardrobe wasn't going to be suitable for Maine weather, even in early September. She hadn't even considered something as mundane as the weather after she'd received the telephone call from Portland late that morning.

She had been stunned when a female police officer had informed her that her sister, Lorrie, had disappeared while working on an island off the coast of Maine.

"Some of her belongings were found at the top of a steep cliff about midday, and one of her shoes on the rocky beach below." The officer added that the authorities were speculating the young woman had fallen or jumped into the rough current, and that her body had been swept out to sea.

Ashley was stunned. "No, I don't believe it."

"I'm sorry. We'll let you know about any further developments."

Not Lorrie! She'd gone to Greystone Island to catalogue some vintage clothing being offered for auction by a wealthy family who owned an estate on the Atlantic side of the island. The Langdons' island property had belonged to the illustrious family since the late 1800s, and they had decided to release a collection of vintage clothing accumulated over several generations.

Lorrie had called from New York, all excited. "I've been hired by a prominent New York auction house to make an inventory and pack the collection for shipment." She'd sounded enthusiastic and confident about the assignment.

During the week she'd been on the island, Lorrie had called Ashley several times with glowing reports about how well the inventory was going.

She couldn't be dead. She couldn't!

They'd always been very close, raised by a widowed mother who provided for her two daughters by working as a seamstress in one of the fashionable New York designer houses. Both girls had grown up with a heightened sense of fashion and color, and both had attended a Manhattan design school. After their mother's death, Ashley had left New York and started a successful business, Hollywood Boutique, specializing in original beaded bags, coin purses, and accessories. Now at age thirty, she employed three women full-time and was kept busy creating intricate beaded designs that bore her trademark. Lorrie had stayed in the New York area, working freelance for museums and auction houses offering vintage apparel.

Now she's missing! Presumed dead!

Ashley had left her shop in the hands of a trusted employee, Kate Delawny, and secured a seat on the first available flight. She had endured several hours of layovers in connecting flights across the country. A sense of disbelief had traveled with her every minute of the journey as she tried to absorb the shock.

Now she stood shivering in the foggy night air. Her ears were filled with the sound of the pounding surf lashing the wharf. Anchored boats in a marina tugged at bowlines like captured animals struggling to get free from their chains. Lights in a nearby parking lot did little to illuminate the empty ferry station or the dark harbormaster's small building with its posted sign for the next day's public transportation. The bay was dotted with numerous crafts looking like ghostly specters on the black surf. There were signs advertising daily water trips—all daytime hours.

Bracing herself against the wind, Ashley walked slowly out on the long pier. She was prepared to pay the price for any kind of transportation. Small fishing boats and larger cruisers tugged their moorings, and pier boards creaked under her feet. She searched anxiously to find someone aboard one of the boats who would respond to her urgent need.

"Hello. Hello. Anybody?" Her voice was driven back down her throat by the wind. Shivering in the clinging moist fog circulating around her, she brushed her dark brown hair away from her eyes as she peered into the mist. She knew that Greystone Island was one of numerous islands lying out there somewhere in the darkness.

I have to get there somehow!

Turning around and bending her head against the wind, she made her way back to where the taxi had left her. A collection of low structures, all dark and deserted, stretched along the water's edge. A strong odor identified them as fish houses. A few neon lights blinked where several weathered buildings clustered together, set back from the waterfront. Bracing herself against the wind, she hurried in that direction.

A renovated warehouse with a swinging sign outside the door identified the place as the Dockside Bar and Grill. Signs in the nautical-shaped windows promised food, drink and music.

Without hesitation, Ashley hurried inside.

A huge, high-ceilinged room was crowded with

people, and a pungent mix of smoke, liquor and sweat instantly assaulted her nostrils.

Loud voices and a couple of strumming guitars blasted her ears. A group of men in work clothes crowded around the bar, laughing and draining their mugs as if all the beer kegs were going to run out soon. A few women sat at tables, smiling and drinking as heartily as their companions.

When no hostess appeared to greet her, Ashley made her way to the first empty booth. She was grateful for the warmth as a bone-deep chill began to ease. Putting her small suitcase on the seat opposite her, she quickly took off her damp jacket and rubbed her arms to restore some circulation. She was thankful that her tailored blouse was still dry, and the pair of casual soft leather loafers had kept her feet from getting chilled.

A blond waitress wearing tight nautical pants and a brief halter suddenly appeared, her pencil poised above her pad. "What's your poison?"

"Coffee," Ashley responded readily.

"Spiked?"

"No. Just black."

"Okay, but you look as cold as a mackerel on ice." The waitress was middle-aged, overweight, and showed that her feet hurt by the way she stood. Glancing at the suitcase Ashley had placed on the vacant seat, she said, "I'd have me a little warm-me-upper if I was you."

Ashley shook her head. "I don't think so."

Even though she needed some help getting through

this nightmare, liquor wasn't the answer. She had to keep focused. No telling what news awaited her on the island.

The waitress shrugged and disappeared into a crowd that was growing every minute. Waiters and waitresses darted about with trays of drinks held above their heads to avoid the crush of customers pressing in on them. Ashley was beginning to think she'd never see her waitress again when she finally brought the coffee.

Ashley thanked her and then asked, "I wonder if you could help me? I need to get to Greystone Island as soon as possible…tonight. It's—it's a family emergency. Do you know anyone who I might hire to take me over?"

"The weather report don't look good," she answered, frowning. "Something's blowing in."

"I know, but, surely, one of these men would like to make some easy money," Ashley insisted. "I'll gladly pay extra."

"I don't know. It's about a forty-five-minute run out to Greystone in good weather. On a night like this…?" She shrugged.

"Please, it's very important."

"It must be," she said as she studied Ashley's pained expression. Then she turned and looked over the men at the bar.

Ashley held her breath.

"Jenkins might do it," she said after a long search. "He's always up for getting his hands on a little more beer money."

"Will you ask him, please?" Ashley's heartbeat quickened.

"Okay, but I still think you'd do better to wait 'til morning." She turned and Ashley watched her make her way across the crowded room to the long bar.

She tapped a burly-looking man on the shoulder. Ashley couldn't see his face clearly under the duck bill of his hat as he turned around and listened to what the waitress was saying. Then he looked across the room to where Ashley was sitting. When she saw him nod and the waitress smile, a wave of relief almost made Ashley giddy.

He's going to do it!

Without hesitation, she agreed to pay the amount he asked after the man had shuffled over. Jenkins had thick shoulders and a ruddy face. He led the way down the wharf to an old motorboat which was probably used to take men out to their fishing crafts.

A dank, fishy smell permeated the air as she stepped down into it. She took the bench seat near the stern, and placed her suitcase at her feet while Jenkins sat on a forward bench, his back to her as he hunched over the motor.

The wind and fog had increased during the few minutes she'd been in the café. Ashley's uneasiness intensified. She debated asking him about a life jacket, but was afraid anything she said to the man might stop him from taking her out to the island.

He threw off the bowline and started swearing when he had trouble starting the motor. The boat began to rock in the choppy water. She couldn't have climbed out if she'd wanted to because the boat was already floating away from the pier.

Maybe the boat isn't even seaworthy!

As the boat swayed in the rising waves and deepening troughs, its old timbers began to groan. When the motor finally caught and the boat lurched forward, Jenkins' slurred muttering and colorful swearing added to the sickening plunge of Ashley's stomach.

Too late, she realized the boatman was drunk!

"Turn back!" she yelled, but her words were driven back in her throat and Jenkins didn't even turn around.

As the motorboat sped forward, dark clouds blanketed the moon and stars, and the mainland was quickly lost from view. Short, choppy waves and buffeting northwestern winds seemed strong enough to capsize the creaking boat.

The mournful tolling of a buoy came closer in the rolling fog. Could he see where they were going? Would they pass Greystone Island in the fog? Fleeting glimpses of scattered watery lights appeared from time to time. Then darkness again. Were they passing all the islands dotting the waters off the coast of Maine and blindly plunging out into the rough Atlantic Ocean?

The nightmare was never-ending. Ashley's stomach took a sickening dip every time the boat fell into a deep trough in the sucking water.

When the throbbing vibrations of the boat beneath her feet began to lessen, she clutched the side of the tossing boat, fearing the motor had given out and that they soon would be adrift in the darkness and fog.

Jenkins suddenly gave a jubilant shout, as though surprised by his own navigation. "There she be! Greystone Cove. Pretty as you please."

Thank God, she thought as watery lights ahead grew brighter and the movement of the boat slowed. Her relief was shattered an instant later.

Jenkins misjudged the landing completely. He hit the pier with a jolt that landed Ashley in the bottom of the drenched boat. Her suitcase and shoulder purse tumbled on top of her.

A man with a deep voice shouted, "You blasted fool, Jenkins. What in blazes are you thinking? Nobody with brains worth two cents would make a crossing in this weather."

Jenkins mumbled something.

The stranger approached the boat and offered a pair of firm hands to help Ashley out of the boat. At the same time, he demanded, "Are you crazy? Hiring a drunken fool to bring you out to the island at night and in this weather?"

She stiffened her shivering shoulders as she glared back at him. "I didn't have a choice."

"You must be reckless—or stupid. You're damn lucky to be on solid ground. I've got a heater in the car." He picked up her suitcase and started down the pier.

She didn't move. She was not going anywhere with this stranger. He was a tall, well-built man, wearing jeans, a knit pullover, a windbreaker and no hat. In the shadowy light, she guessed he was probably in his thirties. He might not be drunk like Jenkins, but he presented another kind of threat.

When she didn't follow, he turned around. "Are you going to stand there shivering all night?"

"Who are you?" she demanded without moving an inch.

Jenkins snickered. "He's a big shot."

"That'll be enough out of you, Jenkins," he said as he walked back to Ashley. "I was just trying to get you out of this weather before the storm breaks, but I should have introduced myself. Brad Taylor, police officer."

"You're a policeman? Where's your uniform?" she demanded. Big-city skepticism instantly flared.

"I'm off duty."

"He's a big shot around here," Jenkins repeated. "Likes to throw his weight around."

Ashley felt an instant rush of relief. She quickly introduced herself. "Please take me to the police department. My name is Ashley Davis. I need to know what's being done to find my sister."

"My apologies. I didn't realize your urgency." As increasing blasts of wind and rain whipped the water, he said, "Let's get in the police cruiser and I'll explain the situation."

"What about me?" Jenkins asked, following them. "Where's my pay?"

"Oh, yes, of course." Ashley quickly drew her wallet out of the shoulder purse and gave him the agreed-upon amount.

"Thank ye." Clutching the bills, he sauntered off, obviously heading for a well-lighted bar near the wharf.

"He's already drunk," Ashley said. "I didn't realize it until it was too late."

"You're damn lucky. We've lost a lot better pilots than him in rough waters like this." He guided her to a police car parked close to the pier. He told her there were only a few cars on the island because they had to be brought in by hired transport. The ferries were passengers only. As he slipped into the driver's seat beside her, she could see shaggy, reddish-brown hair that framed well-defined cheekbones, a strong chin, and an expressive mouth. He was probably darned attractive in a uniform, but thcrc was a scxy toughncss about him that was disturbing. Should she ask to see his badge? What if he had an agenda of his own for offering her his help?

"Do you often patrol the wharf at night?"

"No, I just happened to be down at the wharf when I saw Jenkins ram the boat into the pier," he said as he started the car.

"Has there been any news of my sister?"

He shook his head.

Anxiety made her voice strained. "I want to talk to someone in charge."

"I guess that would be me."

She must have misunderstood. "What?"

"I'm the only law officer on the island."

"No, that can't be."

"I'm afraid it is," he replied firmly. "Greystone Island has a year-round population of only a few hundred people. Granted, in the summer months it doubles, but for the most part, the demands for law enforcement are slight. I can handle it by myself and with my one deputy. But the fact is—"

"That you're not qualified to handle anything serious," she finished in a strained voice. She couldn't believe it! Her sister was missing and there wasn't any qualified police force looking for her.

"You're quick to assume the worst, aren't you?" he replied as his dark brown eyes appraised her.

"I don't hide from the truth in any situation." Her lips trembled. "Not even one as devastating as this one."

"I see." His jaw tightened. "Well, I was about to assure you that I have over ten years of experience as a police investigator for the state of Maine. I've handled almost every kind of crime you want to mention, and I came to Greystone Island a couple of years ago as the resident police officer."

"Why?" Her tone clearly inferred there must have been some impropriety involved in the change of assignment.

"I was raised on the island and for personal reasons wanted to come back," he answered curtly.

"I see." But she didn't. She was too much of a city girl to imagine living on a tiny island that was hardly more than a speck in the ocean.

His jaw tightened. "I've handled your sister's disappearance as I would any case, here or on the mainland. A hunting party was organized to scour the island, radio announcements were transmitted to boats coming and going from the island. My deputy and I circled the island in our patrol boat, but in the enveloping fog and thickening storm clouds, visibility was poor."

"But it's been hours since she disappeared!" Ashley protested.

"I had to call off the search 'til morning," he said firmly.

"Someone must have seen her leave the house."

"Apparently she went for a walk right after breakfast. A fisherman's wife who brings fresh produce up to the Langdon kitchen came upon some of her things at the edge of a steep drop-off and saw one of her shoes at the bottom of the cliff. I was immediately notified and began the search." He backed the car away from the pier and headed along a road leading away from the water.

"I've questioned the hired staff: a housekeeper, a male Asian cook who doesn't speak much English and an all-round housemaid. The rest of the help is hired on a needs basis."

"Yes, Lorrie told me a little bit about it."

"Apparently your sister sometimes took meals with the family, and sometimes she didn't. On occasion, she'd walk down to the Wharf Café for breakfast or lunch, and sometimes had dinner at the Chowder House. After a few days, the household paid little attention to her coming and going. We're fortunate to have discovered her disappearance as soon as we did."

Not soon enough. She bit her lip to keep back the sharp retort.

"I assume you'll want to stay with the Langdons."

Ashley nodded. "If they'll agree to it." They would

know whether or not Officer Taylor was as capable and well-trained as he presented himself to be. She didn't know how to justify her feelings, but she felt more should have been done in the hours her sister had been missing.

"Do you know the Langdons well?" she asked in an even tone as if she'd accepted his explanations.

"I guess it depends on what you mean by know. Of course, everyone on the island *knows* them, but mostly by name and reputation. When I was a teenager, I attended some annual celebrations they sponsored on the lawns of their property, but since my return over a year ago, I haven't had the occasion to be in their company. Until now, with the investigation."

"They stay on the island year round?"

"No. In the summer there's a parade of wealthy visitors who rent the summer cottages on the south-western high cliffs, but after Labor Day they are mostly deserted. Usually the Langdons have left by this time, but for some reason, the elder Clayton Langdon is staying longer than usual."

"My sister told me that his son, Jonathan, is really in charge. Lorrie said he wasn't very friendly. All business."

"I can believe that. Jonathan is fifty and he's been taking over the reins of the family's finances for several years now. His father, Clayton, is a widower in his late seventies. The only woman relative in the house is Ellen Brenden, Jonathan Langdon's late wife's sister, and she's about Jonathan's age."

"There isn't any Mrs. Jonathan Langdon?"

"No. Jonathan's late wife, Samantha, was killed in

an automobile accident some twenty-five years ago. She left a baby girl only a few months old. Raised without a mother, Pamela Langdon grew up spoiled and she died from a drug overdose two years ago, shortly before I came back to the island. She was only twenty-three. Pamela's death was hard on her father and her grandfather."

"I can imagine." Ashley suppressed a shiver. What a tragic family. What kind of ill fate had drawn her sister into it?

As they headed for the Langdon house, the car windows grew foggy, and a narrow dirt road plunged into the darkness of thick trees and huge granite boulders. The pitch of the car told Ashley they were climbing at a steep angle.

The headlights swept across jagged rocks, and spumes of white foam rose in the air. She could tell they were skirting the edge of a steep shoreline. Her nails bit into the palms of her hands as the sound of pounding surf grew louder and louder. A sudden deluge of raindrops splattered in a mesmerizing pattern on the windshield as strong winds whipped them against the car.

"How far is it?" she asked in a strained voice.

"Within walking distance of the wharf," he assured her. "But not on a night like this. The Langdon house sits on the highest point at the southwestern tip of the island. There's a great view when the weather's clear, but its location makes it vulnerable to wind, rain and fierce winters."

Ashley sat rigidly in the seat, staring straight ahead. *Lorrie...Lorrie.*

"Tell me, what exactly was your sister doing for the Langdons?" he asked, which surprised her. Surely he'd been informed of her assignment at the house. She had the feeling he was just trying to keep her mind occupied.

Briefly, she explained the Langdon family's decision to auction some of the vintage clothing that had been collected since the turn of the century.

"A lot of money involved?" he prodded in a slightly skeptical tone.

"A handmade gown by a noted designer can bring as much as a hundred thousand dollars."

He let out a slow whistle.

"Private collectors, dealers and museums are always on the lookout for the kind of vintage clothing that the Langdons have decided to put on the market. Prices have shot up eighty percent in the last five years. There's a charm about antique clothing and jewelry. Lorrie was excited that she was the one chosen to catalog everything." Ashley's voice broke as she remembered how happy her sister had been when the assignment had been confirmed.

"I'm sorry," he said. "We'll get to the bottom of it, I promise."

They both fell silent.

A few minutes later, he swung the car in a half circle and parked at the side of a sprawling, three-story structure that seemed to be balanced precariously on high ground facing the rocky Atlantic shoreline below.

All the windows were dark except for a couple on the main floor. The roar of the crashing surf was like a greedy monster lashing at the land with a crazed fury.

"This is known as the Langdon compound," he explained as he hurriedly guided her along a walk to the front of a white mansion. "There are several outbuildings and a private dock below the mansion."

She straightened her shoulders and brushed damp bangs back from her forehead as they mounted wide steps to a pair of carved doors. She had never felt more unkempt and had never cared less!

"Be careful," he said as he rang the doorbell.

She stiffened. "What do you mean?"

"Just what I said. Watch yourself. There's a pattern of violence in the Langdon family." His tone was hard as the granite rocks strewn along the beach. "Tragedy seems to follow anyone who unwittingly gets snared in their web."

Chapter Two

The front door was opened by a tall, angular woman with gray hair pulled back in a tight knot. She wore a shapeless dark dress that accented her beanpole figure. As she admitted them into the entrance hall, her sharp glance went to their wet shoes; she looked as if she might order them to take the sodden footwear off before allowing them any farther into the house.

"Evening, Mrs. Mertz," Brad said, nodding. He'd met the widowed housekeeper earlier when interviewing the family after Lorrie's disappearance. The austere woman had answered his questions curtly, maintaining she hadn't even been aware of Lorrie Davis leaving the house. Edith Mertz's attitude had given him the impression that she hadn't thought the comings and goings of the young woman were worthy of her attention.

"Will you inform the family that Ashley Davis, sister of the missing woman, has just arrived from California." Brad's tone made it sound more like an order than request.

"They're in the family sitting room," she replied

curtly. "Understandably upset. I certainly hope you will clear this up quickly, Officer. The entire household has been distressed by this unfortunate event." Her tone clearly indicated she thought the island's poor police protection was to blame. "Follow me, Miss Davis."

As she turned away, Ashley shot him a questioning look. Despite all her bravado, he could tell she was looking for his support.

"You want me to stay?"

"Yes, please."

He had decided to leave her suitcase in the car until they knew what kind of reception she was going to get. Clearly accepting guests in their home, unless they were personally invited, was not the norm for a prestigious family like the Langdons; they might expect Ashley Davis to find accommodations elsewhere. Unfortunately, seaside cottages were already closed for the season and only a couple of questionable boarding houses took in transient year-round visitors.

He boldly put a guiding hand on her arm as they followed the housekeeper across a wide foyer. They went past a curved staircase mounted against one wall and then down a hall paneled in dark walnut.

They had passed several closed doors when they met a man, wearing a raincoat and carrying a medical bag, coming toward them.

Brad nodded in recognition of the island's doctor. "Evening, Dr. Hadley."

He was a tall, nice-looking man in his late forties, with graying dark hair and a well-toned body that matched his alert expression. The doctor was Clayton Langdon's private physician, and he handled only routine medical cases that arose on the island. All others he sent to the mainland either by boat or arranged a helicopter pickup at the school playing field. A makeshift ambulance van was kept in the garage of the doctor's home office.

"How is he, Doctor?" Mrs. Mertz demanded in her usual curt manner. "We hated calling you out on a night like this but—"

"No problem," Dr. Hadley quickly assured her. "Clayton is less agitated now, and I left something for a good night's sleep when he's ready to retire." He nodded at Brad. "Evening, Officer. Any new developments?"

"'Fraid not."

The doctor glanced at Ashley. "My goodness, young lady, you look chilled to the bone. You'd better get into some dry clothes and have something hot to drink. We don't need another patient in the house."

"No, we certainly don't," Edith Mertz echoed with pursed lips as if Ashley were bringing some kind of sickness into the house.

"From the sound of that wind, we're in for a night of it." He gave them a brisk nod and continued down the hall toward the front door.

Mrs. Mertz led them deeper into the house and then turned into a brightly lit sitting room warmed by blazing logs in a large fireplace.

Three people sat in chairs near the fire. Brad kept his hand on Ashley's arm as they moved toward them. An elderly Clayton Langdon squinted at them, and his fifty-year-old son, Jonathan, frowned at the intrusion. A slightly built woman, somewhat younger than the men, rose to her feet with the habitual response of a hostess to unexpected guests.

She was Ellen Brenden, the sister of Jonathan's late wife, Samantha, who had been killed in that automobile accident on the mainland nearly twenty-five years ago. Now in her forties, Ellen had become a fixture in the Langdon's household.

Brad liked her. Ellen was a spry and energetic woman with dishwater brown hair cut short around a full face. She wore a colorful, trendy outfit designed for a younger woman. Living with the Langdon family afforded her a comfortable lifestyle, but Brad thought that meeting the demands of the two Langdon men couldn't be an easy row to hoe.

"This is Ashley Davis, the dead girl's sister," Mrs. Mertz announced in her abrasive manner.

"Missing sister," Brad loudly corrected her.

"Oh, yes, of course...missing," Ellen Brenden stammered as if trying to rectify the housekeeper's embarrassing error.

Brad guided Ashley across the room to where Clayton Langdon and Jonathan were sitting. "Miss Davis flew in from California this evening in response to her sister's disappearance," he told them briskly.

Jonathan had quickly risen to his feet. He was a man of medium height and weight, slightly round-shouldered, with a furrowed brow which seemed to reflect heavy responsibilities. As acting head of the family, he looked older than fifty.

"Pleased to meet you, Miss Davis." He offered his hand. "I regret the unhappy circumstances," he added in an apologetic tone.

"Damned confounding! That's what it is," bellowed the seventy-nine-year-old Clayton. As he fastened wrinkle-lidded eyes on Ashley, he clamped his sagging mouth shut and lapsed into a belligerent silence.

"Is there anything new?" Jonathan quickly asked Brad, ignoring his father's outburst.

"Not yet."

"This must be very trying for you, Miss Davis," Jonathan said sympathetically.

"How could such a thing like this happen?" Ashley demanded, worry and bewilderment in her voice.

"Very unfortunate," Jonathan agreed in a people-management tone.

"Just awful," Ellen echoed. "She was…is…a very pleasant and agreeable young woman. All of this is too frightful to believe. What could have—"

"Where is your home, Miss Davis?" Jonathan asked, deliberately interrupting.

"San Francisco. I came as soon as I received the news of her disappearance. It took all day because I had to change planes and make three connections."

Clayton grunted as he leaned forward in his chair. The old man's heavy-lidded eyes reflected a far-off look, but his voice was surprisingly firm. "Traveling is always exhausting under the best conditions, young lady. Even in a private plane you have to contend with all the time changes."

An exasperated look crossed Ashley's tired face. Brad knew her nerves were already threadbare. Trying to cope with mounting anxiety was taking its toll. He quickly intervened.

"Dr. Hadley wanted Miss Davis to have something warm to drink and perhaps a robe around her shoulders."

"Oh yes, a cup of hot tea," Ellen responded quickly. "It's a late hour for coffee, isn't it? Please sit here, Miss Davis." She motioned to a nearby chair and as Ashley wearily dropped down into it, Ellen handed her a knitted afghan.

"Thank you," Ashley said as she spread it over her damp lap and legs.

"I made it myself. Pretty isn't it?"

As if enjoying the unexpected company, Ellen happily gave her attention to a silver teapot and china cups that were already sitting on a nearby small table.

"I was enjoying a cup of peppermint tea myself," she bubbled. "Cream? Sugar? Lemon?"

Ashley just nodded as if making a choice was too demanding. Brad took the cup of tea from Ellen and carefully placed it in Ashley's trembling hands.

"I expect you would probably prefer a highball, Officer Taylor," Jonathan spoke up as if he'd already anticipated Brad's answer.

"I never drink on the job," Brad answered evenly. He'd learned earlier in life that it was better not to socialize with any of the island's wealthy inhabitants.

Even as a teenager growing up on Greystone, he'd viewed the Langdons' social whirl from afar. Since he'd been back, his contact with the parade of wealthy visitors who rented cottages at the southwest tip of the island had been purely in the line of duty. Only the disappearance of a woman in the Langdon household had gained him entry into this pseudopolite rich society.

After taking a few sips of tea, Ashley said firmly, "Now, I would appreciate hearing from all of you anything you can tell me about my sister's disappearance."

"I'm sure Officer Taylor has filled you in," Jonathan responded smoothly. "We know little more than what we told him."

"And what was that?" she asked pointedly.

Jonathan looked at Brad as if he expected him to speak up, but Brad deliberately kept silent. Sometimes people tripped themselves up when they tried to repeat the same story in the same way.

Jonathan cleared his voice. "We have arrangements with one of the local housewives to bring fresh produce and seafood to the house every day. She found a woman's belongings on a cliff not far from here. She brought them to the house, and our housemaid, Clara, recognized them as belonging to your sister. The circumstances seemed dire and we quickly reported her absence."

"It's just too awful," Ellen sighed.

In the weighted silence, Clayton Langdon cleared his throat. Then he barked, "Prepare a room for Miss Ashley. She will be our guest."

Mrs. Mertz shot Jonathan a questioning look. At his

nod, she turned on her ugly shoes and left the room like a soldier with marching orders.

Brad made a mental note to interrogate Mrs. Mertz again. In her position, the housekeeper was bound to know a hell of a lot more about what went on in the house than she had admitted.

"I'll bring in your suitcase and check back with you in the morning," he told Ashley as he prepared to leave.

She cleared her voice and took a deep breath. "You need to ask for help," she said bluntly as her trembling hands held the fragile tea cup. "Surely the Portland police should take some responsibility. They could send someone."

"Like a rookie cop?" he suggested curtly. It rankled him that she had clearly classified him as a local yokel who couldn't find his own dog tied to a post. Without another word, he turned and left the room.

THE BEDROOM the housekeeper had prepared for Ashley was on the ocean side of the house. The sound of the surf assaulting the rocky cliffs could be heard above wailing gusts of wind. By the time Ashley had followed Mrs. Mertz through a complex of halls and curved staircases leading to the second floor, she was totally disoriented. The rambling mansion seemed to be a weird maze of rooms and additions to the main structure throughout the years. The housekeeper stopped at the far end of a long hall and opened a bedroom door.

"We've already closed up this side of the house for the winter," Mrs. Mertz informed Ashley without any hint of an apology for the cold and musty smell inside the room.

A large bed with a massive wooden frame stood against one wall, and an old-fashioned chiffonnier matched a free-standing wardrobe and vanity. Even though the furniture was rather massive, there was an air of youth about the faded decor on the walls and the feminine furnishings.

In addition to the overhead light, there was a bedside lamp. Ashley's small suitcase sat in the middle of a faded, fringed rug; she assumed that a servant must have brought it up earlier.

"Would you like me to turn down the bed?" Mrs. Mertz asked with a glint of amusement in her eyes.

Yes, please, and bring a hot water bottle to warm the covers, Ashley retorted silently. She wished she had the courage to play the spoiled socialite guest and order a housekeeper around.

"I put out an extra comforter and turned on the heater in the bathroom. Is there anything else?"

"Where does that door lead?" Ashley asked, pointing to a door flanked by two tall windows on the ocean side of the room.

"The widow's walk. It's a long narrow balcony that runs the length of the original section of the house. Amelia Langdon, the first mistress of the house, is reported to have paced it night and day, hoping for some sign of her husband's clipper ship coming back from trade in the Indies. This was the master bedroom then."

"I see."

The housekeeper's thin lips curved in a faint smile. "Amelia's lonely watch never brought him back that last time. His ship was wrecked at sea. Some say she's still waiting and watching. Sometimes on moonless, stormy nights, the poor lady's ghostly form has been seen walking right outside that door."

"Really? How exciting. All these old mansions have their own delightful ghost stories, don't they?" Not for all the world would Ashley let the housekeeper spook her. "Thank you for your help, Mrs. Mertz. I appreciate it."

"Good night, then," she replied in a tone as crisp as burnt toast.

Ashley closed the door after her and then leaned against it, struggling to control her emotions. She wanted to cry and scream and throw things. Never had she felt so close to being totally out of control. Slightly panicked, she drew in long, shaky breaths to steady herself. It wouldn't do herself or her sister any good if she fell apart.

She bit her lip, straightened her shoulders and went into the small adjoining bathroom. It had obviously been renovated; the fixtures were modern, and the tile was an expensive mosaic pattern.

She stripped off her damp clothes, turned on the shower and held her breath until the spray changed from cold to a satisfying warm temperature. Grateful for scented soap and shampoo, she showered and washed her hair. As she dried herself, she caught her reflection in a gold-framed mirror above an oval-shaped sink. Worry and fear were etched in her face. Yesterday she'd been immersed in the challenges of her business. Now the success of Hollywood Boutique seemed hollow.

Lorrie. Her sister's name caught in her throat. Tears eased out of the corners of her eyes. *I'm here, Lorrie. I'm here.*

THE STORM passed over during the night. Ashley thought she must have slept a bit, even though she had twisted and turned restlessly. She was aware that sometime in the night, the rain had stopped and the wind had died down. Darkness outside the door and windows began to lighten to a dull gray. She got out of bed and dressed quickly in designer jeans, a cotton blouse and a jacket.

Despite Brad Taylor's assurance that he'd put out information on her sister's disappearance, Ashley decided she wasn't going to sit and wait for him or anyone else to respond. Her pent-up emotions demanded release. She was convinced that somebody on the island knew what had happened to Lorrie. She'd brave the chilly, foggy morning and walk down to the wharf. People might feel freer talking to her. She really didn't care whether Officer Brad Taylor liked it or not.

Cautiously she opened her door. With only a vague idea of how to find her way out of the house, she began walking down the gloomy hall. All of the doors along the corridor were closed and there was no hint of anyone occupying the rooms. She must have covered the entire length of the wing the housekeeper had said was closed before she came to a narrow staircase that descended rather steeply to a closed door at the bottom.

She hesitated. Were these the same stairs she'd climbed last night? No, they were too narrow and steep.

Was it going to take her half the morning to find her way out of the house? She knew it was early. The only sound she heard was the whisper of her steps and the creaking of the dark planked floorboards. High, gabled windows let in rays of feeble early sun. Maybe the household would not be stirring for hours.

When she came to a carpeted hall that widened, she sensed a difference in the surroundings. The musty smells disappeared as she hurried forward. When she came to another staircase, she thought it was probably the one she'd climbed the night before.

She peered over the banister and searched for a glimpse of something familiar in the hall below. When she reached the bottom of the steps, her ears picked up a clatter of kitchen noises and her nose sensed the odor of cooking.

She turned in the opposite direction. Her choice turned out to be the right one. She found herself in the front foyer. The heavy front door echoed loudly in the early morning hush as it closed behind her.

Drawing her jacket closely around her, she headed down the narrow road through a dark tunnel of trees that had hugged Brad's car on both sides last night as they had driven up from the wharf. Wisps of gray fog rose from needled spruce branches drooping heavily with moisture. The road followed the rugged shoreline, and salty moist air bathed her face.

Slowly, the wooded area gave way to ground vegetation, and as the road descended from the high point of the island, she could see scattered weathered buildings near the wharf. There was a bustle of movement along the pier. Men were loading their boats for a day's fishing and hauling on the water.

Ashley hurried to the small, whitewashed Wharf Café. Once inside the door, she was assaulted by the warmth of bodies, a clamor of loud voices and stares from the male customers.

She was out of her element and she knew it. Approaching these strangers was a far cry from relating to city merchandise buyers, but she was desperate. Moistening her dry lips, she began to circulate through the crowded tables. As she explained who she was and pleaded for any information about her missing sister, a ripple of quiet began to descend on the café.

"My sister was working for the Langdons. She's a blonde, small and—"

"We know," an older man with gray whiskers interrupted.

A rough-looking fisherman nodded. "Nice gal. Came in here once in a while for lunch, she did."

"Heard about her disappearance," offered a woman in work clothes sitting at one of the tables.

Ashley's anxious gaze traveled around the room. "If anyone has any idea about what could have happened to my sister, please tell me. Anything...anything, at all."

"Officer Taylor's been all over the island," a gruff man boomed.

At that point, a young waitress hurried over to Ashley. "I'm so sorry about your sister. Lorrie's always so friendly and nice. I just love waiting on her." She pressed Ashley's hand. "She has to be all right...she just has to be! I can't believe—" She broke off as someone came into the café. "Brad! Any news?"

"Not yet, Betsy." Brad's eyes settled on Ashley. "You're out early, Miss Davis."

"Yes, I am," she replied, keeping her head erect and squarely meeting his eyes. "I thought I'd meet a few people on my own. Just in case—"

"I missed something?"

"I just want to help."

"Good. I'm just heading to the office to make radio contact with as many boats in the area as I can. Would you like to come along?"

The invitation surprised her. Being at the heart of the investigation was better than letting her imagination run wild.

"Yes, I would. Thank you. I'll call the Langdons and let them know where I'll be."

"Have you had breakfast?" When she shook her head, he turned to the waitress. "Betsy, send a couple of breakfast specials and coffee over to the station."

BRAD WAS SILENT as they walked a short distance to a municipal building that also housed a volunteer department and the island's post office.

He had no idea why he had impulsively invited Ashley Davis to come to the office with him. Something in her dogged manner had surprised and rather pleased him. He wouldn't have expected her to have that kind of determination and self-sacrifice. His annoyance at her lack of faith in his abilities had been tempered by a begrudging admiration. He wasn't used to having a woman challenge him on any level, but as she matched his step and walking rhythm, he suspected he might have found one.

"This is it," he said as he ushered her inside. He wasn't about to make apologies for its stark ugliness. The Greystone police station amounted to two rooms: an office and a small, windowless back room that served as a temporary jail. More often than not, the cell was occupied by someone needing a place to sleep off a hangover. The boatman, Jenkins, had been a guest more than once.

"Sorry, the place is a mess." He quickly cleared a chair of a pile of folders. "I was attempting to clean the files when the Langdons called about your sister. Have a seat. Coffee and breakfast will be here soon."

She surprised him with an apology. "I'm sorry if I was out of line going to the café like that. I just couldn't stay at the house and wait."

"No harm done. I'll get started on the radio calls." He turned his back to her and sat down at an old desk.

"Isn't there something I can do to help?" she asked, still standing.

"Not at the moment."

She fell silent as she sat down in a chair behind him. She picked at the breakfast order when it arrived, but Brad barely touched his, only pausing for hurried sips of black coffee.

He kept on the radio, referring to a record of various

craft that had listed call numbers with the Portland authorities. He asked each commercial and private pilot to relay any information that might help locate the missing woman.

As the minutes ticked by, he could sense Ashley's frustration as she began to move restlessly around the small office.

Welcome to police work. Tedious, boring and exacting.

His own exasperation was at a high level when an urgent call came in from a fishing boat heading out into deep Atlantic waters.

"We weren't sure what we were seeing," the captain said after giving his location. "Looked like something floating loose and the closer we got, we could tell it was an old rowboat. We weren't equipped to chase and snag it, but we got close enough to plainly see it. I'll be danged if there wasn't a woman lying in the bottom of it."

"We're on it!" Brad signed off and hurriedly paged his deputy. "Get the patrol boat ready to go out, Bill. We've got a lead."

He'd forgotten all about Ashley, until he swung around and saw her standing behind him with a face as white as an Easter lily.

"Is it—?"

"Maybe. Let's go!"

He grabbed her hand as they raced to the pier.

Chapter Three

Brad was at the wheel of the police cruiser, and Ashley and the deputy at the bow of the boat when they headed down the western coast of the island and out into the open waters of the Atlantic.

Stocky, round-faced Bill Hunskut kept a pair of binoculars focused on the water ahead as he firmly planted his thick, muscular legs on the rolling deck. Ashley guessed him to be a little older than Brad.

Ashley was oblivious to the cold mist of water spraying her face as she clutched the railing with both hands. Her body was rigid and her pulse rapid as they searched the rising and falling waves for a drifting rowboat.

The sky was clearing after last night's storm. Patches of glistening sunlight reflected in the rising and falling gray-blue water were creating illusions. Her heart leaped into her throat when she saw a floating object in the water.

She pointed and cried excitedly, "There! There!"

Deputy Bill gently touched her arm. "It's only a floating porpoise, miss."

Sometimes it was floating debris or a weathered log that made her chest tighten. With every tortured minute, the hopelessness of finding a tiny boat in a vast sea grew greater and greater.

Lorrie. Lorrie. Her sister's name was a mantra on her moist lips when the deputy suddenly yelled.

"Starboard! Starboard!"

As Brad quickly swung the boat in that direction, Ashley squinted but couldn't see anything.

"Where? Where?"

Bill pointed, and her breath caught as a rolling wave brought the floating object into view.

"There it is!" Brad quickly slowed the cruiser's speed. "Get the hook ready." With exacting patience, he began to maneuver the cruiser close enough for Bill to try to snag the rowboat.

Ashley clenched the railing with white-knuckled hands. The motion of the police boat kept moving the floating boat away.

Finally, after several frustrating tries, Brad succeeded in bringing the old boat alongside.

Ashley hung over the railing. When she saw her sister's crumpled, still body lying in the bottom of the rowboat, knife-like pains shot through her.

No, no! She can't be dead.

Both men moved with quiet competence. They lowered a rope ladder so that Brad could descend into the rocking boat. With his strong arms, he put the inert body into a carrier sling fastened to a pulley from above.

Ashley realized what a well-trained team they were to handle such an emergency.

At Brad's signal, Deputy Bill raised the sling to deck level. Once it had been lowered onto deck, both men instantly knelt beside the litter. Blond hair was matted with blood from a swelling at the back of the young woman's head, and her arms and legs were motionless.

"Is she…?" Ashley choked.

Brad checked for vital signs, searching for a pulse in the limp wrist and laying his head on her chest to detect any faint movement.

"She's alive. Get the oxygen ready, Bill. Only a very faint pulse, but we may have a chance."

He carried her into the cabin, which had been equipped with first aid emergency supplies, and quickly laid her on a stretcher-like cot.

"We've got to get her warm." He turned to Ashley. "Get some blankets out of that cupboard. Bill, set up the oxygen tent. I'll radio the Portland stationmaster to have an ambulance ready. We can get her to the mainland quicker than returning to Greystone and summoning a helicopter to pick her up."

The trip was the longest one Ashley had ever made. The minutes crept by as she kept her eyes glued on Lorrie, watching for any sign of consciousness. Almost imperceptibly, Lorrie's deathly color began to change in the oxygen tent. The feeble sound of air moving in and out of her chest told Ashley she was breathing deeper.

"Reckon we found her in time," Deputy Bill

encouraged in his calm, homespun way. "She'll be fit as a fiddle, you wait and see."

An ambulance was waiting on the wharf when Brad eased the patrol cruiser into its assigned berth on the mainland. Immediately, two male paramedics came aboard, took charge, and transferred Lorrie to the ambulance.

"We'll follow in my car," Brad told Ashley. "I keep one in a nearby parking area for use when I'm on the mainland." He told Bill to arrange for the rowboat to be examined for forensic evidence. "You catch the afternoon ferry back to the island, Bill, and I'll call in as soon as we know something."

ASHLEY SANK BACK in the seat of Brad's compact car and stared ahead as he drove in silence to the community hospital. She was grateful he didn't try to engage her in conversation. Apprehensive and emotionally drained, she was functioning at a precarious level. His firm, solid and unruffled manner helped steady a hurricane of feelings whirling within her.

When they reached the hospital, they hurried into the emergency room. Brad used his official status to gain assurances that as soon as any news was available, he would be immediately advised.

"I'm afraid there's nothing to do but wait," he told Ashley as they turned away from the desk. "I need to make some calls. I'll be as quick as I can. Would you like to have me bring you back some coffee?"

She shook her head and swallowed hard. For a

moment, she had the absurd urge to insist that he didn't leave her.

As if reading her thoughts, he said, "I'll only be a few minutes, I promise." He gave her a quick squeeze on the shoulder, turned and disappeared down a nearby hall.

She found an empty chair in the crowded room and sank down into it.

AS BRAD made his way to a small office he'd used before when conducting business from the hospital, he was puzzled why he felt so personally involved in this investigation. He'd handled plenty of traumatic situations when he had been an investigator in the State Enforcement Bureau. Plenty of heart-rending tragedies. Plenty of attractive, appealing women. What was it about Ashley Davis that made everything about this one different? Was it because she'd stood up to him and openly questioned his competence? Just this morning in the café, she'd even been trying to do his job.

"Dammed if I know why she gets to me," he muttered to himself.

He called his superior in Portland and brought him up to date. "I don't know how soon I'll be able to question the victim. She's in emergency now, and we're waiting to hear if she makes it." They talked for a few more minutes.

When Brad returned to the emergency room, he waited with Ashley. It was nearly noon when a young doctor gave them the news.

"She's conscious and her condition is stable." He told them she'd been moved to a private room. "You can see her for a few minutes."

LORRIE'S EYES were open when they entered her room, and her lips curved in a weak smile as Ashley bent over and kissed her cheek.

"You had me scared, Loribelle," she said, using a pet name.

"Sorry, Sis," she whispered weakly.

"You're going to be all right. The doctor says so." She motioned Brad to come closer to the bed. "This is Officer Brad Taylor."

"Nice to meet you, Lorrie." He bent over the bed and smiled down at her.

Lorrie stared up at him and then said weakly, "Big one, isn't he?"

Ashley chuckled. Leave it to Lorrie to say whatever came into her mind. At that moment, for the first time since the horrible nightmare began, she truly believed her sister was going to be all right.

"Could I ask you a few questions, Lorrie?" Brad asked politely in a nonthreatening tone.

"It's all fuzzy...like a bad dream," she said in a tremulous voice. "What happened...what happened to me?"

"Someone knocked you out and put you afloat in a boat," Brad answered evenly. "Lorrie, do you know anyone who might want to harm you?"

In a weak voice, she whispered, "Maybe Sloane."

"Why Sloane, Lorrie?"

Ashley could tell Brad knew who Lorrie was talking about, but before her sister could answer, a nurse interrupted them.

"You have to leave now. Doctor's orders."

"Can't I stay with her?" Ashley protested.

"All you would do is watch her sleep," the nurse answered briskly. "Come back tomorrow. She'll be ready for a visit."

"It's okay, Sis," Lorrie mumbled weakly. "Tell the Langdons—"

"Don't worry about the inventory," Ashley said. "I'll work on it until you're well." Her background and experience in textiles was strong enough to satisfy the auction company.

She kissed Lorrie's cheek and blinked back tears as they left the room. She felt totally drained, but as they made their way out of the hospital, anger began to surface. "Who is Sloane?"

"A drifter. Comes and goes. Works the lobster boats sometimes. Makes just enough money to keep himself in drink and cheap food." Brad clenched his jaw. "He's bought himself a pile of trouble this time if he's the one who did this."

"You'll arrest him?"

"If there's any evidence he's guilty."

"Lorrie said it was Sloane!"

"No, she said it could have been Sloane," Brad corrected her. "That's a big difference from saying she knew for certain he was the one who knocked her out and set her adrift in the rowboat."

"Who else could it be? My sister doesn't go around making enemies."

"I promise I'll check on Sloane, up, down and sideways. If he's the one, he'll pay plenty for this attempt at murder."

"And if he isn't?"

"We'll just have to keep looking."

A HEAVY SILENCE engulfed them as they headed back to the island. Brad was lost in his own thoughts. Ashley was weak with relief that her sister had been found alive; that miracle crowded out everything else.

It was midafternoon when they docked the patrol boat.

Brad said, "I'll drive you back to the Langdons'."

"Thank you, but I'd rather walk," Ashley replied quickly. "I need some time to myself. You know, digest everything that's happened." Her voice choked. "Thank you for finding Lorrie...saving her life...and everything."

"You're the one with courage," he replied gently. "I wish I had a sister who would turn the world upside down for me if I was in trouble." As if surprised by what he'd said, he added briskly, "I'll keep you posted."

She walked quickly past the cluster of buildings dotting the area around the wharf and started back up the road she'd walked that morning.

Now that the fog had lifted, she could see summer cottages hugging the shoreline and nestled in wooded areas. Most of them seemed deserted.

The moanful cry of a loon seemed to follow her as she made her way along the high bluff where the Langdon mansion rose against the sky.

As she approached the front door, it opened suddenly and an athletic-looking man dressed in slacks and a Norwegian knit sweater came out. When he saw her, his mouth curved in a pleasant smile.

"Miss Davis?"

She nodded with a slight questioning lift of her eyebrows. Thick, dark, slightly gray hair framed a strong, masculine face. She guessed him to be somewhere in his mid to late forties. A diamond ring flashed on his hand as he reached out to shake hers.

"I'm Paul Fontaine," he said, introducing himself. "My law firm handles Mr. Langdon's legal affairs."

She nodded, surprised that he was a lawyer. He didn't seem to fit the stereotype of the legal profession. He was dressed too casually and his manner too effusive.

"The family was just telling me you were here and about Lorrie's disappearance. I didn't know. I've been busy on the mainland for a few days. I only chatted with the young lady a couple of times. Is there any news?"

"Yes, we found her!"

"Alive?"

"Yes, she's in the hospital. Thank God, she's going to be all right."

"Wonderful. The family will be delighted. I can't wait to see their faces." He added, quickly, "They're in the family room."

Ashley had no idea where the family room might be in the maze of halls and connected rooms. "I'm not familiar with the house."

"It takes some getting used to," he admitted with a slight chuckle. "I still get lost sometimes."

"You stay in the house?" she asked, wondering why she hadn't seen him the night before.

"No," he responded, shaking his head. "I use the guest cottage when I fly in from New York for a conference with Clayton and Jonathan." He lowered his voice. "Frankly, it's a break from the office routine, and I like to do a little deep-sea fishing when the weather's good. They loan me one of the cars to get around the island and I was just about to drive down to the wharf. But I'm in no hurry. Come on, I'll show you the way to the family room."

Ashley tried to keep her bearings but she became lost as they passed through connecting doors, adjoining rooms and down a series of short halls. When they finally descended down some wide steps and entered a high-ceilinged room with large windows, she was surprised to find herself in a pleasant sitting room that opened onto a terrace.

In contrast to the rest of the house, the room was light, and airy, and she could see why the two men and Ellen had gathered there instead of in last night's formal drawing room.

Fontaine broke the news to them before Ashley had a chance. "They found her. Alive!"

Ellen cried, "Oh, dear Lord!"

Old man Langdon leaned forward in his chair. "What…what?"

Jonathan strode across the room and searched Ashley's face as if he were afraid to believe Fontaine. "Where?"

Ashley took a deep breath and sat down in the closest chair. As unemotionally as she could, she told them about the rescue. "Lorrie was knocked out from a blow to the head. She's weak from being out in the wet and cold, but she's regained consciousness and the doctor says she's going to recover."

"That's wonderful," Ellen bubbled.

"Did she say who was responsible?" Fontaine asked.

Ashley decided not to mention Sloane. Brad had made it clear there had to be some evidence of the man's guilt before an arrest could be made.

"Lorrie doesn't know," she responded truthfully. "Apparently, she was stuck from behind and never saw her assailant."

"Maybe she'll remember more when she gets better," Ellen offered.

Clayton Langdon made a wheezing sound. His color was a pasty gray as he put his bony hand on his chest and sucked in air.

Ellen was on her feet immediately and rushed over to his chair. "Oh, dear, too much excitement."

The old man quivered like a strangled bird struggling for air and seemed to hover on the edge of unconsciousness.

"Jonathan, call Dr. Hadley," Ellen ordered. "Your

father's having another attack." She summoned Mrs. Mertz and sent her after his medications.

The drama was too much for Ashley. While everyone clustered around Clayton, she followed the housekeeper out of the room.

"Where do I find my sister's room and her workroom?"

"They're across the hall from your room."

"And where is that?" Ashley asked in exasperation.

"Take the stairs," Mrs. Mertz replied briskly over her shoulder and disappeared down a hall.

"Great," Ashley muttered as she climbed narrow, steep stairs that ended at a closed door. Only feeble light illuminated the passage.

The door creaked as she opened it, and she gingerly stepped out into an unfamiliar corridor. As she looked up and down, closed doors along the way gave no hint of what might lie behind them. The faint echo of the ocean's surf reached her ears, and she headed in that direction. When she came to descending stairs that resembled the ones she'd taken that morning, she knew where she was.

Ashley decided she'd better get a handle on the inventory as quickly as possible. When she reached her room, she turned to the door directly opposite hers and gingerly opened it. Peering in, Ashley felt a rush of warmth.

Lorrie's usual clutter was spread out all over the bedroom. A lovely sight. Ashley smiled. Never again would she chide her sister about her messy habits.

She found two empty suitcases and began to pack up her sister's belongings. She'd take them to the hospital tomorrow, so they'd be there when Lorrie was ready to leave.

After she'd finished packing, she looked around the room to see if she'd missed anything and noticed a door on the inside wall next to the closet. It opened to an adjoining room. Judging from the casual furniture and curtained windows overlooking the water, she suspected it had been a sitting room at one time with a second door that opened out into another hall. She'd found Lorrie's workroom. No doubt about it. Vintage apparel and accessories were everywhere. A variety of garments hung on racks, others were sorted in piles and some still lay in opened old trunks. The assortment was mind-boggling.

The collection included beautiful Edwardian gowns of satin, lace and taffeta. In addition to a myriad of day dresses fashioned by famous designers, there were flounced petticoats with ribbons and edging, and shawls that reached the floor with silken fringes.

On a worktable, Lorrie's meticulous cataloging was evident in her lists of items and a file of accompanying photos she'd taken. Various accessories, such as purses, scarves, silk flowers, and ornate jewelry, seemed to be packed and ready for transport.

Everything in the room possessed a kind of mystique that totally charmed Ashley. She felt strangely drawn to the women who had owned these beautiful things. Sensuous silken fabrics and lingering scents seemed familiar to her, as if in another lifetime she might have worn the satin gowns and ornate necklaces that had circled their necks. The impression was fleeting, but uneasiness remained. As she looked around the room, she sensed an undefined warning.

Satisfied that she could continue where Lorrie had left off, Ashley returned to her bedroom and was surprised to find a housemaid just finishing making up the large canopy bed.

A quick-moving, blondish young woman had straightened up the bathroom and had hung Ashley's few clothes in the wardrobe. She'd even laid out her makeup and brush set in an orderly manner on the vanity.

Ashley quickly apologized. "I'm sorry. I left in a hurry this morning. I don't want to trouble you every day to make the bed and—"

"No trouble. I'm Clara." She had a pleasant smile, and Ashley judged her to be in her early thirties.

"I'm glad to meet you, Clara. And thank you."

"I've always liked doing this room. It's nice to have somebody in it. I used to set it right every day." Her tone grew pensive. "Don't know why they've left it all shut up for so long. I'm surprised Mrs. Mertz decided to put you here."

"It's a spacious room," Ashley commented and wondered what there was about it that lacked warmth.

"Pamela liked it."

"Pamela?"

"Mr. Jonathan's daughter. You should have seen the room then. She had all kinds of bright pictures on the walls and knickknacks everywhere. She had everything any young woman and bride-to-be could want when she had this room." Her voice faltered. "She died...two years ago now."

"Yes, I heard about the tragedy." She remembered Brad had said the young woman had died of a drug overdose.

"I'd been her maid since I came to the house. She was always so full of life. I couldn't believe it. Only twenty-three years old. Her wedding dress was hanging in the closet. I'd pressed it the day before. I know she never meant to kill herself, even though she and her fiancé had a big fight. He stormed off and Pamela shut herself up in this room..." Clara's voice petered out.

"What a tragedy," Ashley murmured gently.

The maid reached out and smoothed a coverlet on the bed. "I found her...right here...in this bed. All cold and lifeless." Her voice thickened as she turned and stared at Ashley. "I wonder why old lady Mertz put you in her room? She always hated my Pamela."

Chapter Four

As Ashley stared at the bed, her imagination began to taunt her with haunting impressions. A young girl lying on the bed...drawing her last breath...clutching the pillow with desperate hands—

Stop it! Her nerves were threadbare enough without giving in to morbid fantasies. The housekeeper probably had a pragmatic reason for putting her in this room. After all, it was across the hall from the one Lorrie had occupied and close to the workroom. That made sense—didn't it? Maybe, but from the moment Mrs. Mertz had opened the door, it was obvious to Ashley that her presence wasn't welcome.

BRAD WAS on the wharf when the returning fleet of fishing boats pulled into the harbor after a full day's run. The air was redolent with the smells of fish as tired crews began unloading their catch for the day's tally.

After asking around, Brad had learned that Sloane had gone out with Old Man Whitkins, who had trouble keeping any kind of a permanent crew because of the pittance he paid. The crusty old codger had to depend on unreliable help like Sloane, who signed on when he needed drinking money.

Whitkins's old boat was one of the last to come into view. Brad saw Sloane sitting on the deck, his feet propped up on a lobster cage while he smoked a cigarette. He heard Whitkins yelling at him to cast the bowlines as the fishing vessel prepared to dock.

Brad decided to wait until Sloane had finished unloading the boat before he approached him. He didn't want to cheat Whitkins out of any work he was paying the man to do. As soon as Sloane headed toward the pub with his wages in his hand, Brad fell into step with him.

"Looks like you had a good day's catch," Brad commented.

"How in the hell would you know?" Sloane growled. "When's the last time you put your hands into a smelly lobster trap?"

"I deal in other kinds of smelly business," Brad answered as he put a detaining hand on Sloane's arm. "I have some questions that need answering. Either here or at the office. What's your choice?"

Sloane's body stiffened and Brad was prepared to block a sudden uppercut and land one of his own, if need be. Sloane seemed to read Brad's readiness.

"What the hell is this about?"

"Lorrie Davis."

A slight flush deepened Sloane's suntanned face. "That city bitch. What about her?"

"I hear you made some unwelcome advances and she brushed you off."

Sloane cursed. "She had her nose too high in the air to see a good thing. No wonder she ended up missing."

"Did you have anything to do with that?"

"Hell, no!"

"Where were you the day she went missing?"

"On Whitkins's boat. I've been out every day this week with the old buzzard. He wouldn't pay me until our run today. You can't pin this one on me, copper." Sloane smirked. "I hear you've got her sister in tow. How's that working out for you?"

Brad controlled an urge to spread Sloane's sneer all over his face and settled for giving him a rough shove backwards. "I'll be checking out your alibi. Don't leave the island. I'd hate to have the mainland police detain you in one of their cozy cells while I do some very, very slow paperwork."

Sloane answered with foul-mouthed muttering as he stalked away and disappeared into the crowd of rough men pouring into the saloon, ready for some strong drink and loud talk.

Brad silently swore. Whitkins would undoubtedly confirm that Sloane had been out with him since early morning the day of Lorrie's assault. He wished he had better news for Ashley. He braced himself to tell her they were still on square one with no leads as to who had wanted to kill her sister.

AFTER A SHOWER and a change of clothes, Ashley made her way down to the family parlor just before dinner time. She chose a navy daytime dress of woven Georgette and added her knit jacket for warmth. Now that she knew she was going to be staying on the island for at least a couple of weeks, she'd need to do some shopping in Portland for some weatherwise clothes.

She made several false choices in the maze of corridors before she found the right stairway down to the first floor and the family sitting room. Ellen was there, chatting away with a young man who sat on the sofa beside her, a drink in his hand.

At Ashley's appearance, he quickly set down his drink and rose to his feet as his gaze traveled over her.

"This must be Ashley Davis," he said before Ellen had a chance to introduce them.

"And this is my nephew, Kent," Ellen said quickly, smiling broadly. "He pops in now and again to say hello."

"Nice to meet you, Kent," Ashley responded politely, trying to ignore a sudden dislike for the smiling, deeply tanned Kent. She judged him to be in his late twenties. Tightly stretched knit pants and a shirt hugged his muscular forearms and thighs, and he had an indolent air about him. "Do you live on the island, Kent?"

"Nope. Just passing by."

"A friend of Kent's has a yacht he brings up from Long Island," Ellen explained. "They have a great time with young people partying on the different islands. Sometimes he spends a few days with me." She added wistfully, "When he and Pamela were growing up, he was here a lot."

Ashley eased down into a chair opposite the sofa. “I just learned about Pamela’s tragedy. I understand I have her room.”

“I guess Mrs. Mertz thought you’d want to be close to the workroom, like your sister,” Ellen offered.

“Hey, that’s good news that they found her,” Kent said, resuming his seat. “Do they know what happened?”

“Not yet,” Ashley answered evenly. “Had you met Lorrie, Kent?”

Ellen answered before he could. “Oh, yes, they had a couple of nice chats. Kent was telling her about some of the good times he and Pamela had growing up together. She was only a baby when my sister, Samantha, was killed in an automobile accident. Jonathan needed help raising her, so I came to live with the family.” Her voice faltered. “Pamela was like my very own.”

Ashley was ashamed of herself for wanting more details, but the weird way she’d been drawn into the tragedy made it seem very real to her. “An accidental death, was it?”

“Hell, yes,” Kent swore. “Pam wouldn’t take her own life. She was in a snit over the blowup she and Timothy had and got careless. Timothy stomped off and left her. He was with us on the yacht all night. Didn’t hear about her overdose until morning.” He stood up. “I need another drink.”

Ellen glanced at her watch. “There isn’t time, Kent. You can have wine with dinner. We’ll be eating in the family dining room. I understand that Paul Fontaine is going to join us.”

Kent groaned. "Deliver me! I'll grab something from the kitchen to eat on my way out."

Ellen looked disappointed but didn't argue. He stood there waiting as she reached into her sweater pocket, took out an envelope and handed it to him.

"Thanks, Auntie." He quickly kissed her cheek before he turned to Ashley. "See you around."

Not if I can help it, Ashley silently vowed. To all appearances, he was a spoiled young man who sponged off his aunt. Pamela's tragic end seemed to have had very little effect on his partying lifestyle.

"Shall we join the others?" Ellen asked as she rose to her feet and smoothed her bright burgundy sweater-dress, obviously designed for a taller, younger figure. A silk floral scarf and dangling ruby-colored earrings accentuated the roundness of her full face.

Ashley was grateful that she didn't have to find the family dining room the first time on her own. It seemed to be in another wing of the house and she heard the creaking of an elevator descending when they reached a wide hall.

When the elevator door opened, Clayton Langdon shuffled out slowly. Dr. Hadley was at his elbow and when he saw Ashley he said, "I heard the good news about your sister, Miss Davis. I hope she's doing well."

"Yes, thank heavens."

"The poor girl is at Community Hospital," Ellen spoke up, not about to be cut out of the conversation. "And Ashley is going to take over the inventory."

"By whose authority?" Clayton croaked.

Ashley kept her tone even. "I'm sure you'll find my credentials adequate to finish Lorrie's assignment, Mr. Langdon, if that's your desire. If not, you can notify the auction house to send someone else."

"Clayton, you don't need any more stress," the doctor spoke up. "I don't understand why you insisted on burdening yourself with such a project in the first place. Be grateful to Miss Davis. Hopefully, she can finish it as quickly as possible and you won't have to concern yourself with it any more."

"He's right, Clayton, dear," Ellen chimed in as if she couldn't pass up an opportunity to throw in her two cents' worth. "You need to spend your energies on your health. Doesn't he, doctor?"

Clayton muttered something under his breath and continued to shuffle his way into the dining room where Jonathan and Fontaine were standing, talking in low tones. Both men turned and greeted the elder Langdon.

"Will you join us for dinner, Dr. Hadley?" Ellen inquired politely. "I'm sure we can set an extra place."

"Thank you, but I have another call to make. One of the dock workers has an injured hand that needs some attention." There was a tired slump to his shoulders as he shifted his medical bag and walked away.

Ashley was sorry he'd refused the dinner invitation. She felt more comfortable with him than with the other men. As she entered the spacious dining room, Paul Fontaine moved forward to greet her.

"We meet again," he said tritely as he held out a chair for her next to his.

An elaborate chandelier hung above a table set with polished silver, porcelain dishes and hand-cut glasses. As soon as the five of them were seated, Mrs. Mertz gave a signal to Clara and another serving girl to move forward. During the meal, the housekeeper kept her eagle eyes on their every movement.

For most of the meal, the conversation centered on topics introduced by the three men. Ashley exchanged a few words with Fontaine when he asked her some questions about her use of the Internet to market her original boutique designs.

"I would love to learn how to bead," Ellen commented, having unabashedly eavesdropped on their conversation. "Would you teach me, Ashley?"

Ashley silently groaned but kept a smile on her face. "If I have time. There's quite a bit of work to be done before the inventory is complete."

After dinner, Ashley excused herself. "It's been a long day. I believe I'll turn in."

"Of course, dear," Ellen agreed. "Have a good night's sleep. We'll see you in the morning."

She left them in the main drawing room and was heading for the stairs when she heard Brad's deep, resonant voice down the hall from the front foyer.

Quickly she turned and headed in that direction.

BRAD THANKED the maid for letting him in and was surprised when Ashley suddenly came into view. From the anxious, expectant look on her face, he knew she wanted some news about Sloane. She'd already made it clear enough she expected Brad to arrest the man and charge him with the crime.

If only it were that easy.

He'd better have a private talk with her. "Where's the family?" he asked.

"The living room," she replied. "We just finished dinner. Clayton's lawyer, Paul Fontaine, is here."

"Are you warm enough for a walk on the terrace?"

At her nod, he opened the front door, took her arm and guided her around the north wing of the house to a wide covered terrace facing the ocean and the cliffs below.

The house was dark on this side. Party rooms with French doors opening onto the terrace were closed up. At the height of the summer season, multicolored lights from the house could be seen five miles out on the ocean, but in cold weather, like a hibernating creature, the house lost its warmth and color, standing stark still upon dark granite rocks.

When Ashley shivered, he knew she had pretended to be warm enough. He quickly took off his jacket and put it around her shoulders.

"Don't argue. Your teeth will be chattering in a minute. Maybe we should go back inside."

"No," she said firmly. "I'd rather freeze."

"Well, I'll try to see that doesn't happen," he said drily.

Hugging his jacket around her, she asked, "Did you find Sloane? Is he in custody?"

He took a deep breath. "Yes and no. Yes, I met him when came in on a lobster boat late this afternoon. No, he's not in custody."

"You let him go!"

"He has a rock-solid alibi. He couldn't have possibly assaulted your sister. I've verified he left early that morning on Whitkins's fishing boat and worked as a deck hand 'til dusk."

"But Lorrie said—"

"I know. Sloane probably hassled her and that's why she said his name. If your sister wants to press charges for any harassment I'll pick up Sloane. For more than that, I can't arrest him."

Worry lines deepened in her face. "What do we do now?"

"I'll follow every possible lead. Maybe Lorrie will remember something else...someone else. I promise you I'll not waste a minute looking for the person responsible."

She looked so small and fragile huddled down in that mammoth jacket of his that he stiffened against the urge to envelop her in his arms and hug her against his chest. "How are things going with you and the Langdons?"

"All right, I guess. I learned today that Mrs. Mertz put me in Pamela Langdon's old room." Her voice caught. "I'm sleeping in the same bed where she died."

Brad swore. "Damnit, you don't have to put up with that!" He suspected the housekeeper was sadistic as hell. He'd heard tales of the way the housekeeper treated the staff. So far, he hadn't been able to learn whether she and Lorrie had had any kind of a confrontation.

"Were you on the island when Pamela committed suicide?" Ashley surprised him by asking.

"No, it happened shortly before I came back to Greystone as a police officer. Pamela was just a baby when her mother, Samantha Langdon, was killed in an automobile accident. I guess her father, Jonathan, and her aunt, Ellen, had their hands full raising her. Apparently, Clayton Langdon doted on his granddaughter and spoiled her. She was only twenty-three, ran with a wild crowd and was engaged to some guy everyone considered a pothead."

"That's what the housemaid, Clara, told me."

"It's not a nice story and I'm sorry you had to hear it right now." He put an arm around her shoulders "I'll make damn sure you get better treatment from now on."

"No, I don't want to make waves. I'm afraid the old man has already half decided not to let me finish Lorrie's assignment. My sister is depending on this project to bring in some money. I can't let her down."

"Maybe we could find another place for you to stay. One of the other cottages…or mine?"

Mine! Stunned, he couldn't believe what he was saying. He guarded his privacy like a hermit, and he didn't even know this woman. How had she managed to slip past the emotional reefs that guarded against any personal involvement with the opposite sex?

Fortunately, she was shaking her head. "I'll be fine. It's better that I stay in the house. It'll save the time of coming and going."

They walked over to a waist-high brick wall that overlooked stone steps leading to a boathouse, where a long pier extended out into the water. No sign of any boats anchored there. Ashley remarked how dark and deserted it looked.

"Does the family use it?" she asked.

"Jonathan's younger brother, Philip, had it built to accommodate his yacht. Now and then he makes dutiful visits to see his father," Brad explained. "Philip's the complete opposite of Jonathan. Good-looking. Man about town. Lives off his investments. Been married and divorced three or four times."

"Are there any grandchildren?"

"Jonathan's daughter, Pamela, was the only one."

"That's sad."

Ashley remained in the circle of his arm as they turned away from the water and walked a stone path bordering the sprawling mansion. A few scattered ground lights spread a yellowish glow on the dark grounds.

"I think that's my room up there," she said when they reached the original part of the house.

"How do you know?"

"See the high narrow porch? Mrs. Mertz said my outside door opens onto a widow's walk. Apparently there are tales about the early days when—"

He followed her gaze as she stopped short. "What is it? What do you see?"

Dark eaves and gray windows rose to a slanted roof as uncertain moonlight put the house in shadow.

After a long minute, she stammered, "Nothing... nothing." Then she gave an embarrassed laugh. "For a moment I thought I saw a figure on the widow's walk. It must have been my imagination."

Chapter Five

Ashley thought she'd glimpsed a moving form against the backdrop of the widow's walk. But even as her eyes had transmitted the image to her brain, it had disappeared.

As they moved closer to the house, she scanned the second story. No sign of any presence there—ghost or otherwise. She sighed as a wave of fatigue swept over her.

"You need to get some rest." He gave her shoulder a gentle squeeze. "Come on, I'll see you inside."

They entered the house through the nearest side door, which happened to be near the family room. Even though a couple of lamps were turned on, there was no sign of anyone there.

"I can find my way from here," Ashley told him.

"Are you sure?"

She nodded. "I've used the back stairs that go up to the second floor." She handed him back his jacket. "Thanks for coming tonight."

"I'll keep you updated on any developments," he

promised. "Meanwhile, don't be wandering around the island by yourself."

"I'll be taking the ferry to visit Lorrie in the afternoon. I'll be working here at the house all morning. I've got to get a handle on what needs to be done to finish up Lorrie's assignment."

"Before I leave tonight, I'll have a talk with Jonathan and make sure you're treated all right." He paused and added in a softer tone, "Will you call me if you need to talk with someone? This can't be easy for you."

She met his eyes squarely. "Lorrie's alive. I can handle anything else."

"Yes, I believe you can." A slight smile tugged at the corners of his mouth. "I'll see you upstairs now."

She could tell from the set of his head and shoulders that it wouldn't do any good to argue. In a way, she was grateful for his insistence as he accompanied her up the steep staircase and down the shadowy second-floor hall.

The door to her bedroom was open and a small bedside lamp she'd left on gave a welcoming warmth. Even as she started to tell him goodbye, he came in and crossed the room to the outside door.

She realized then why he had insisted on seeing her to the bedroom. Whether he believed her vision or not, he had intended to check out the widow's walk for himself.

"Is this door always unlocked?" he asked as he opened it.

"I don't know," she answered honestly. She hadn't paid any attention to it in the short time she'd been there.

As he stepped outside, Ashley watched him from the doorway. He quickly walked the length of the empty widow's walk from one end to the other. *He must think I'm really paranoid,* she thought as he came back into the room and slid a dead bolt in place.

"Keep the door locked."

"Thank you for checking."

"That's my job," he replied briskly. "Now, I'll sec if I can find my way to the front of the house."

"Good luck."

"Keep this locked, too," he ordered as he paused in the hall doorway.

For some impulsive reason, she gave him a snappy salute. "Yes, sir."

She was certain he was quietly laughing as he turned and disappeared down the hall.

ASHLEY WAS SURPRISED at how well she slept that night. Even before she had thrown back the covers and stood up the next morning, her mind was already busily prioritizing. First, she'd call the hospital and make sure Lorrie was all right. Then she'd have breakfast and spend a busy morning in the workroom. After lunch, she'd take a ferry ride to the mainland.

She chose a pair of peach-colored jersey slacks and matching top she'd brought because they packed easily. Not exactly fitting for a misty Maine island, but there was a promise of clearing skies and maybe a warm September sun.

Ellen had told her there were three telephones in the

house: one in the front foyer for general use, another in the kitchen for household business and the third in a study that both Clayton and Jonathan used as an office. Unfortunately, the island was not set up for any cell phone transmission.

"We're lucky to have private phone service at all," Ellen had told her. "For years, there was nothing but party lines. Believe me, nothing was private with all the eavesdropping going on."

Ashley decided that privacy wasn't much better for the phone in the foyer. It sat on a corner table with a lady's chair beside it, and anyone in the hall or the adjoining rooms could easily monitor any phone conversation. Ashley decided if she needed privacy, she'd use the public phone in the café.

She called the hospital and was told Lorrie had spent a restful night. They were still keeping her lightly sedated, but she could have visitors later in the day.

Ashley had just hung up when Ellen appeared beside the table, smiling and asking, "How's your sister? Can she have visitors?"

"Only family," Ashley replied.

They walked together down the hall to a small eating room where breakfast had been set out on a buffet. Ellen told her Jonathan and Fontaine had had an early breakfast, and Clayton was having his usual tray in his room.

"He has a night nurse who stays with him until after breakfast," Ellen told her.

Ashley selected French toast, a slice of melon and

coffee. Ellen decided to have a second cup of coffee and keep her company.

"Did Officer Taylor have any news last night? One of the maids told me he was here," she added in a slightly peevish tone. "I guess he only wanted to see you."

Ashley decided she might as well tell her about Sloane. Ellen was bound to hear from someone that Brad had interrogated him as a possible suspect.

"My goodness," Ellen exclaimed. "Your sister never said anything to me about any of the locals giving her a hard time." She acted as if her feelings were somehow hurt that Lorrie hadn't confided in her.

"I expect she didn't want to worry you, Ellen," Ashley said in appeasement.

"Well, Officer Taylor will get to the bottom of all of this. We're lucky to have someone like him on the island."

"Have you known him a long time?" Ashley asked casually, sipping her coffee.

"Goodness, yes. His parents had the mercantile store until they retired and moved inland. Of course, he was never in Pamela's crowd of young people. He went to high school in Portland and then joined the state police force. Came back to the island a couple of years ago as its police officer when Old Man Whitcomb finally retired from the job. We were all glad to see a young, capable policeman take over. Brad Taylor is a fine-looking man." Ellen raised a questioning eyebrow. "Don't you think so?"

Ashley smiled at the obvious attempt to get her to make some personal comment. "I suspect Brad Taylor doesn't lack for female attention."

"I'd say not, especially from the local gals. Someone said they saw him in Portland a few times with different dates. Apparently, he hasn't found anyone who wants to settle year-round on a cold, windy island."

"Maybe he's not the marrying kind."

"Everyone's the marrying kind when they find the right person," Ellen offered philosophically.

"Maybe so," Ashley replied. She wasn't sure why she'd never made it to the altar in her long-time relationship with a man who'd suddenly married someone else. For several years, Owen Prentice had been more of a comfortable steady date than anything else. She'd always refused to move in with him and now she sincerely hoped he'd be happy with his new bride.

After breakfast, she excused herself and made her way back upstairs to the room where Lorrie had been working before she disappeared. Ashley was astonished at the collection of vintage clothing that had come from the wardrobes of Langdon women. Some of the gowns dated from the early nineteenth century. Many had designer labels like Vionnet, Poiret and Schiaparelli. Considering modern-day prices, Ashley knew there was a fortune in these ball gowns made of silk, taffeta, satin, lace and chiffon. Many of them were embroidered with pearls and crystal beads. Her hands trembled slightly as she handled them.

She checked Lorrie's inventory, and carefully placed every garment her sister had already recorded in a long narrow packing box, ready for transport. As far as Ashley could tell, Lorrie's clothing entries tallied perfectly. Her sister had taken pictures of beaded purses, delicate scarves, silk flowers and hair trimmings. The ornate jewelry was mostly costume: cameos, brooches, pins and necklaces. No precious stones. As she checked each item off the list and placed it in an individual box, she discovered she was one item short. Lorrie had listed a gold locket on a narrow chain and had taken a photo of it.

Ashley looked over every inch of the worktable, on the floor under and around it, but failed to find the missing locket necklace. She was on her knees, half under the table, when she heard footsteps outside the door. Before she could make it to her feet, the door opened and Jonathan Langdon stood there, looking down his rather prominent nose at her.

Ashley got to her feet as gracefully as she could and pretended she'd dropped the jewelry photo. She wasn't about to tell him she couldn't find one of the jewelry pieces. Lorrie might have set it aside for some reason.

"Is there some problem, Miss Davis?" he asked as if her manner was less than reassuring.

"No, not at all," she replied quickly and pointed to the stack of packed boxes. "I have those ready for transport and will continue to inventory every item as I unpack the remaining trunks." She gave him a reassuring smile. "I'm impressed, Mr. Langdon, with the condition and quality of the collection."

His expression remained composed but there was a hint of emotion in his voice when he said, "Both my late wife, Samantha, and my daughter, Pamela, were fond of wearing period clothing whenever the occasion arose.

If you run across any photographs taken at various parties, I don't want them included in the collection," he said firmly.

"No, of course not. You can check the complete inventory before you sign the release."

"How long will it take to finish?" He frowned as he looked around the cluttered room.

"I'm not sure," she replied honestly. "It depends on the amount of clothing and items to be handled, photographed, logged and packed. You can rest assured I'll complete the inventory as quickly as possible."

He gave a quick nod of his head. "Well, then, I leave you to get on with it. I want to double-check everything before it leaves the house," he said as he glanced down at the tray of jewelry.

Ashley stared after him as he left the room. Something in the way he'd glanced at the tray of jewelry made her think he might have viewed it earlier. *Had Jonathan Langdon taken the necklace for some reason?*

She worked steadily until noon, then quickly changed her clothes and hurried down to the wharf to catch the one o'clock ferry. She had time to buy a sandwich and drink at the Wharf Café and take it with her to eat on the trip across the bay to the mainland.

She sat down on one of the side benches on the top deck and had just taken a bite of ham and cheese sandwich when she saw Brad standing at the bow of the ship, talking to one of the ship's crew. He must have come aboard at the last minute.

Her reaction at seeing him was a complete surprise.

She'd thought herself well past the age of quickening breath and heartbeat when viewing any member of the opposite sex. But as she swallowed the bite of sandwich and brushed a paper napkin across her lips, the joy at seeing him couldn't be denied. Even as she willed him to turn and look at her, he disappeared into the pilot's wheelhouse, and she was left with a strange sense of abandonment.

She waited for him to appear again, ready to move in his direction if necessary to catch his attention, but the ferry docked at the mainland and she made her way off the boat without seeing him again.

She took a taxi to the hospital and was surprised to find a security guard posted outside Lorrie's room. Brad hadn't told her he'd arranged for one. *Was her sister still in danger?*

Lorrie smiled weakly when Ashley came in and placed a kiss on her pale cheek. "How ya doing, Sis?"

Lorrie's eyes were heavy-lidded, and was obviously being sedated to keep her rested. "Mostly sleeping."

"Good. We'll talk a little and then I'll sit by the bed and listen to you snore."

She gave a faint chuckle. "I guess I still snort a little."

Ashley squeezed her hand. "I've started on the inventory. You did a great job, Lorrie." She paused, debating whether or not to mention the missing necklace. If there was a simple explanation why it wasn't with the other jewelry pieces, she'd like to know it, but decided against saying anything. She didn't want her sister worrying about it.

"What about Sloane?" Lorrie asked, interrupting Ashley's train of thought.

Ashley shook her head. "The guy was working on some lobster boat at the time you were assaulted. Officer Taylor interrogated Sloane and checked his alibi. It has to be somebody else."

Lorrie closed her eyes and her lower lip trembled. "But who? And why?"

Ashley didn't pretend to have an answer.

"Is this Officer Taylor any good?"

"He's been in police work quite a while, working out of Portland until a year or so ago. There's something about him that makes me think he can be trusted."

Lorrie raised a sleepy eyelid. "I never thought I'd hear you mention a man and trust in the same sentence ever again. What's going on, Sis?"

"Nothing's going on. I just happen to think Brad knows what he's doing. He comes across as dedicated, reliable and is—"

"Physically attractive as hell," Lorrie finished.

"Well, yes," Ashley admitted, hoping the heat rising in her neck didn't show. "More importantly, I believe he's determined to uncover the truth, no matter what."

"If only I could remember…"

"We'll find the bastard, Lorrie," she said, squeezing her hand. "Right now, you just concentrate on getting well. I know Ted and Amy would love to have you spend some time with them in L.A. when you're ready to leave the hospital."

"I hate to put you out like this."

"I can handle it, but I'll admit living with the Langdons is a bit of a challenge," Ashley admitted. "By the way, the family lawyer, Paul Fontaine, asked about you. He said you'd spent a little time together."

"He was at the dinner table a couple of times, that's all," she said tiredly. "Seems nice enough."

Ashley patted her hand. "Enough talk."

Lorrie closed her eyes and Ashley stayed by her bedside for another hour while she slept. Before she left the hospital, Ashley found a public telephone and made a couple of long distance calls. She checked in with Kate Delawney and was assured that inventory was adequate to fill new orders for Hollywood Boutique coming in every day. Ashley hung up relieved, and thankful she had someone capable like Kate to take over for her.

Her second call to Ted and Amy, who had been friends of the family since Ashley and Lorrie were children, was equally successful. They would be delighted to have Lorrie stay with them while she recovered from her ordeal.

"You come, too," Amy invited. "This can't be easy for you, Ashley. I'm appalled that such a horrible thing could happen. Please, be careful, Ashley. I think you should get off that island as soon as you can."

"I agree," Ashley answered and promised to keep her informed.

After leaving the hospital, she took a cab to a business district near the wharf and shopped while she waited for the late afternoon ferry. Her purchases included a couple of sweaters, a lined jacket, and two pairs of warm slacks. She found a pair of walking ankle boots that she liked and added them to her list. She decided she could always use the warm clothes if she spent any vacation time in places like Lake Tahoe.

She was just boarding the ferry with her arms full of purchases when she heard a familiar deep voice behind her.

"Did you leave anything in the stores?"

She turned around to see Brad grinning at her. Her foolish heart quickened, but she masked her pleasure. "What are you doing riding the ferry? I saw you on the way over."

"You did?" He looked surprised.

"Yes, you looked—busy."

"I was, but I'm not now." He guided her to one of the benches.

"Why aren't you using the police cruiser?" she asked as they settled themselves.

"Deputy Bill needed it to check with people on some of the nearby islands. I'm hoping there might have been someone in the area when Lorrie was assaulted and perhaps noticed something that would help. I've been busy checking with crews of registered boats coming and going to the outlying islands."

"Any luck?" She knew from the tightening of his chin what his answer was going to be.

"Not a damn bit." He shook his head. "There's got to be something we're missing."

"Lorrie feels badly that she can't be more help." Ashley told him about her arrangements to send her sister to California as soon as she was released.

"Good idea. The sooner we get her away from here the better." He turned to face her. "You, too, Ashley. I'd rather have you leave now, this afternoon."

"I can't. I have to finish the inventory."

"Why?"

"Lorrie's future assignments may depend upon it. I won't let her down."

"I don't suppose it would do any good to try and reason with you. You obviously have a stubborn streak a mile wide."

"So I've been told," she admitted with a wry smile.

"Until I get a handle on this investigation, you'd be better off anywhere but here," he argued. "We don't know what triggered the attack on your sister. You could stumble into the same kind of jeopardy without even realizing it. I don't want to chance it. Leave now, Ashley." He glared at her. "That's an order."

She suppressed a smile at his official demeanor. If he thought she was the least bit intimidated by his brisk, police manner, he was way off base.

"Thank you for your concern, Officer," she answered in a docile tone. "I'll be happy to leave as soon as I've finished."

When they reached the island, he offered to drive her up to the Langdon house in his patrol car. She was about to accept when she heard someone calling her name. Turning around, she saw Paul Fontaine coming toward her. Apparently the lawyer had been in the Neptune Bar when the ferry pulled in. He smiled broadly as he waved.

"You're just in time to catch a ride up to the house," he said as he reached her. "I thought you might be returning about now. I'm using one of the Langdon cars."

"I guess that will save you a trip," Ashley said, hoping Brad would object. She was disappointed when he didn't.

"I'm glad Ashley had such an official escort from the mainland," Paul said. "We're all a little concerned about her wandering around by herself. Have you made any progress in the investigation, Officer? Any possible suspects?" Fontaine prodded.

Brad's jaw tightened. Obviously, Fontaine wasn't high on his list of favorite people, she thought. The negative energy between the two men was as apparent as a lit fuse.

"There's no shortage of suspects," Brad answered curtly.

The lawyer's eyes narrowed. "Well, I guess that's better than coming up empty. We're all very much concerned that the guilty party be arrested as quickly as possible." He turned to Ashley and inquired politely, "How did you find your sister?"

"She's improving."

Brad touched Ashley's arm. "Take care."

Without even a polite nod at the lawyer, Brad strode across the pier and disappeared into the Rockcove Café. Ashley was tempted to ditch Fontaine and join him, but Brad's departure hadn't been anything close to an invitation.

"Abrupt son of a gun, isn't he?" Fontaine commented as he escorted her to a late model, small, compact car parked nearby. "He doesn't mix socially, at least not with the summer crowd or families like the Langdons, but I guess he gets along with the islanders all right. You have to wonder why he'd be willing to be stuck on this island year-round."

Ashley eased into the front seat of the car without answering. His criticism of Brad rankled, even though she'd entertained the same kind of skepticism when she'd first met him. All that had changed, and she ignored a warning that it might not be for the better.

As they drove along the cliff road, the late afternoon sun created moving sculptures as the ocean surf rose and fell. In one of the inlets, a flock of birds dove in the water for their evening meal.

Fontaine seemed oblivious to the surrounding beauty as he launched into a detailed harangue about the dwindling economy of Maine's islands. When they reached the Langdon compound, he took a narrow road below the main house where a guest cottage and small garage had been built on a lower slope. A flight of steep steps led upward to a door on one wing of the sprawling mansion.

"I prefer the cottage to the main house," he said as he opened the door for her and she slipped out with her packages. "I think I do, too," Ashley replied honestly.

A wide veranda on the cottage offered a clear view of the island's shoreline on the eastern side. As Ashley's gaze traveled across large bay windows, she glimpsed a woman with blond hair standing there.

"I'll see you to the house," Paul said quickly and put a guiding hand on her arm as they mounted the cement stairs. "The family room is just around the corner of this wing at the ocean side."

Ashley didn't argue. They passed a number of doors which gave few hints as to which part of the house they belonged. It wasn't until they were on the other side of the house that he stopped and opened one for her. She still didn't know where she was until they reached a familiar staircase in the hall outside the family room.

"Thank you, I can find my way from here."

"Goodbye, then. I'll see you at dinner," he said politely and then quickly made his way back down the hall and out the door. His haste made Ashley wonder who was waiting for him.

When she reached her bedroom, she found it just as she had left it. She threw her purchases on the bed and glanced at her watch. Yes, she could get in an hour's work before it was time to go downstairs for dinner.

When she reached the open door of the workroom, she was aware that someone was moving around inside. She stepped into the room and saw Mrs. Mertz was standing at the worktable, going through inventory sheets and labeled photos. A quick glance around the room verified that many of the packed boxes had been moved and some of the trunks had been opened.

Ashley's temper flared. No telling what harm had been done to the fragile, yellowed garments handled by hasty rough hands. And what was worse, the woman might be responsible for removing items from the collection before they were catalogued.

Drawing in a deep breath to control her fury, Ashley sharply asked, "Looking for something, Mrs. Mertz? Something like a vintage necklace, perhaps?"

Chapter Six

Mrs. Mertz's dark eyes bit into Ashley's face as she replied haughtily, "Mr. Jonathan asked me to check on things."

"Why?"

"There's too much of value here to leave to chance," the housekeeper replied as if the best defense was indeed a strong offense.

"I see. My integrity is being questioned, is that it?" Ashley asked, each word dripping with ice. "Or maybe this is a set-up? Could it be, Mrs. Mertz, that you, or someone in the house, has an interest in some of the items that might bring the most money on the market?"

Mrs. Mertz drew herself up. "I resent your insinuations, Ms. Davis."

"And I, yours, Mrs. Mertz," Ashley replied just as forcefully.

"Very well," the housekeeper said stiffly as she put down the inventory sheets on the worktable. "Mr. Jonathan asked me to relay a message to you. He would like to see you before dinner in his private study. You can tell him yourself about your reluctance to honor his wishes."

The woman's narrow lips curved in a satisfied smile. Then she turned and marched out of the room, her back ramrod straight.

BRAD HAD WATCHED Paul Fontaine and Ashley drive away and disappear up the narrow road. He'd had plenty of run-ins with lawyers during his years on the mainland, and men like Fontaine always rankled him, especially when they stepped on his toes. Even though he wanted to deny it, sweeping Ashley away like that right under his nose was definitely personal. He couldn't even lie to himself and claim his own interest in her was purely professional. Every time he saw her, he was aware of her arresting blue eyes, the appealing softness of her dark hair and the way her lips parted when she smiled. Somehow she had broken down all his barriers against any romantic involvement, and he knew what that meant—trouble!

"What's the matter, boss?" his deputy asked Brad when he came into the office. "You look ready to wrestle a bear to the ground. Any luck today?"

Brad shook his head and dropped down into his office chair.

"Me, neither. I couldn't find a single islander who'd been anywhere near the waters where we found the rowboat." Bill's round, ruddy face creased in a frown. "Nobody knows anything."

"Somebody knows something," Brad countered. "Maybe we're looking in the wrong place."

"What do you mean?"

Frowning, Brad said, "We've been expending our energies trying to get a handle on this thing by concentrating on what happened a few days ago."

"So?" Bill replied, obviously puzzled. "After all, that's when the crime occurred."

"What if there's something malignant inside the Langdon compound that festered up and Lorrie got caught in it?" Brad proposed thoughtfully.

"What are you getting at?"

"I'm not sure," Brad admitted. "But at the moment, I'm ready to try a long shot. Let's look at it this way. We know that there have been two tragic deaths in the family, Jonathan's wife, Samantha, and his daughter, Pamela."

"Both of them accidents."

"So it would seem," Brad said. "Samantha was killed when her car went off the road on the mainland during a bad storm, and the daughter was found dead in her bed from a presumed accidental lethal amount of drugs and alcohol."

"So what's to investigate?" Bill asked skeptically.

"Maybe nothing," Brad conceded as he reached for the phone. "But I think I'll have headquarters send me over some files."

AFTER MRS. MERTZ had flounced out of the workroom, Ashley debated whether she'd been telling the truth. Was Jonathan Langdon really checking up on her? Why hadn't he said something earlier? Had something in her behavior alerted his suspicions? Steaming over the implication that she had to be watched to make sure she didn't make off with some of the merchandise, Ashley was ready to take on Jonathan Langdon and anyone else who questioned her honesty.

She had no idea where his private study might be. Better ask someone, she decided, instead of wandering through the maze of halls for who knew how long. Hurrying downstairs to the main floor, she found Clara in the dining room setting the table for the evening meal.

"Oh, Mr. Jonathan's study is in his suite of rooms on the second floor, west wing," she said. "Just take a left at the top of the main stairway, and keep going until you come to a large sitting room. His study is the door on the left. Just knock."

"Thanks," Ashley said, relieved that Clara's directions seemed rather straightforward. She mentally thanked the maid when she found the study without any detours.

Her brisk knock was followed by a curt, "Come in."

She took a deep breath as she opened the door, ready to state her objections to having someone monitor her work. If it hadn't been for Lorrie's investment in the job, she'd have walked away from the whole project.

Jonathan was sitting behind a desk placed in front of a bank of windows facing the mainland. He stood up at her entrance and nodded.

"Mrs. Mertz said you wanted to see me," Ashley said in what she hoped was a congenial tone.

"I thought it time we had a private conversation," he said in his usual sedate manner.

"Yes, I think so, too," she replied just as formally.

"Let's sit over here." He motioned to two chairs and a coffee table at the other end of the room.

Above the fireplace was a large portrait of a woman in a familiar ivory chiffon and lace ball gown Ashley had recently packed for shipping. Her dark hair was swept up in a high fall of hair, with long ringlets framing her face. Ashley was stunned: she recognized the locket necklace around the woman's neck. Her breath caught. It was the same one that had disappeared from the jewelry inventory!

Jonathan must have mistaken her reaction for artistic appreciation because he explained, "It's a remarkable portrait of my late wife, Samantha. I didn't know she'd secretly commissioned the portrait until after her death." He swallowed hard as if trying to deny a surge of emotion. "Unfortunately, she lost her life in an automobile accident before she could give it to me."

"She's lovely," Ashley said, using the present tense because there was so much life in the beautiful eyes, mouth and figure. Samantha seemed to be smiling at them as they stared up at her radiance. Ashley could understand why Jonathan had never married again. To have such a woman in his life must have diminished the possibility of his marrying anyone else.

"Shall we sit down?" he asked politely, motioning to the chairs. "I know you've been away for the afternoon. How is your sister?"

"Improving," Ashley responded. "I've arranged for her to stay with friends while she recuperates."

"Sounds like a wise decision."

Cutting off any more polite conversation, Ashley plunged into the matter of Mrs. Mertz's presence in the workroom. "Imagine my surprise to find her checking the inventory lists and examining contents of boxes and trunks that have not been opened before. May I ask why?"

"Did you ask her?" he responded as if the fault of any misunderstanding lay with Ashley's handling of the situation.

"She said that she was overseeing the inventory at your request. Apparently you have some concern about my integrity, Mr. Langdon?"

"No, not at all, Miss Davis," he quickly assured her. "I've already had my lawyer, Mr. Fontaine, run a background check. He has assured me that you are a very responsible and successful businesswoman. I apologize for my housekeeper's misinterpretation of my directive. I simply asked Mrs. Mertz to be of service in the completion of the inventory." He sighed. "I had no intention of her trying to supervise you. Please accept my apologies."

Ashley wasn't going to settle for an apology. "I don't need or want Mrs. Mertz's help or presence," she said firmly.

"I understand, but when I checked the room after Lorrie was injured, it was obvious to me that completion was going to take a lot longer than planned. My father is the one who has been insisting that you take over." He leaned forward. "You don't have to continue with it, Miss Davis. It's just an old man's nostalgic whim."

"I promised Lorrie—"

"We'll gladly pay for the time your sister has invested in the project."

On an intuitive level, an unspoken message came through loud and clear. *He doesn't want me to finish it.* Why?

"We will gladly pay for any expenses you've incurred thus far."

"I appreciate the offer, but I'm confident I can finish the entire inventory sooner than expected. If your father is set on offering the collection to the public, we wouldn't want to disappoint him."

After a heavy pause, he agreed, "No, of course not. My father doesn't take disappointment well."

"Will you advise Mrs. Mertz that her help isn't needed?" At his nod, she added, "And I would appreciate it if no one else handles any of the items."

Maybe the housekeeper had been in the habit of snooping through the collection even when Lorrie was in the house. Even as the thought crossed her mind, a possible explanation for the necklace being missing occurred to her. Mrs. Mertz could have taken it! Undoubtedly, the housekeeper would recognize it as the one in Samantha's portrait. She might be the kind to bolster her own feelings of inadequacy by secretly possessing something that had belonged to the late Mrs. Jonathan Langdon. Or maybe Jonathan had taken it himself? She knew he had been in and out of the workroom. In any case, Ashley decided to keep mum about its disappearance until she'd finished the inventory.

"Please don't hesitate to inform me if any problem arises," he told her in an obvious tone of dismissal.

Returning to the workroom, she immediately gave her attention to some of the boxes that Mrs. Mertz had opened. One contained a variety of wide-brimmed ladies' hats that flaunted huge ostrich feathers or clusters of velvet flowers in swirls of ribbon bows and streamers. Another hatbox was filled with various styles of blond and brunette false hair, some in pompadour style, chignons, and others in lengths of flowing tresses.

After laying everything out on the worktable, she carefully photographed and itemized each piece. By the time she'd finished, it was the dinner hour.

She groaned when she looked at her watch. She was too tired to clean up and go downstairs. Then she remembered Ellen saying that sometimes Lorrie had chosen to have a tray brought up when she was working. Ashley wasn't quite sure how her sister had managed it. She looked around for an intercom but didn't see one anywhere.

At that moment, fatigue overrode her need for food. She returned to her room and stretched out on the wide bed. The family would be at dinner for at least another hour. She'd better wait until they'd finished before setting out to find some food. Sighing, she closed her eyes and began to relax.

She must have been asleep for about an hour when she was awakened by a firm knock on her closed door.

"Yes?" she croaked sleepily as she sat up.

Clara poked her head in. "I brought you a tray," she

said, coming into the room. "Miss Lorrie used to expect one when she didn't come down for dinner. I thought maybe it was the same with you?"

"Oh, yes, Clara. Thank you," Ashley said, gratefully. "I wasn't looking forward to making a safari to the kitchen."

"Mr. Fontaine was asking about you," the maid said as she set the tray on a bedside table.

"Oh?"

"He thought someone should check on you, but Mr. Jonathan told him you were working and didn't want to be bothered. I don't think the lawyer liked it much," Clara admitted. "He kinda flushed, you know what I mean? Sometimes he and Mr. Jonathan really get into it."

"About what?"

Clara shrugged. "Who knows? I guess Mr. Fontaine dated Jonathan's late wife, Samantha, before they were married. The old man usually puts a stop to their arguing. I don't think Mr. Jonathan really likes being on the island. He's ready to close up the house and get back to New York. Luckily the staff's got a job here year-round. Takes us all winter to get the place ready for spring and summer visitors."

"I can believe it," Ashley responded.

Clara chatted for a few more minutes before leaving, obviously reluctant to go back downstairs to Mrs. Mertz and her iron-fist supervision.

Ashley enjoyed a delicious meal of breaded chops, creamed asparagus and a baked potato, and then finished a carafe of coffee with a warm piece of caramel apple pie. It took all the energy she had to get up, shower and get ready for bed. Once settled in bed, she thought she wouldn't stir until morning.

It was after midnight when a brush of cold air on her face jerked her awake. For a moment, she was completely disoriented. Even as she sat up and blinked to adjust her eyes, a blur of white and silver swept past the open bedroom door.

The memory of a ghostlike figure on the widow's walk instantly brought Ashley out of bed and into the hall. As the wispy figure moved quickly down the shadowy corridor, Ashley stubbornly darted after it. More than anything, she wanted to validate her own senses. She wasn't imagining! She wasn't dreaming!

If she'd had a better handle on her surroundings, she might have navigated the labyrinth of halls and rooms quickly enough to overtake it. But as she raced through the darkened house, trying to keep the apparition in sight, the distance between them lengthened.

Suddenly the specter seemed to float down a series of twisting stairs, and Ashley lost sight of it. She bounded down after it and found herself at a dead-end staircase. No exit. No sign of the figure.

Where had it gone?

A sudden bone-deep chill replaced the fiery heat of her pursuit.

Chapter Seven

Brad arrived at the Langdon house about lunchtime. He'd called Ashley earlier and told her he was going to the mainland that afternoon. She accepted his offer to drive her to the ferry.

He'd been busy that morning lining up an appointment with a retired officer, Jim Mayberry, who had investigated the automobile accident that killed Samantha Langdon. After going over the official report he'd received from Portland police headquarters, he still wasn't satisfied.

Police investigations had changed a lot in some twenty years, and sometimes "cold cases" turned fiery hot when new evidence revived them. Brad was hoping that a face-to-face rehashing of the accident with someone who had been on the scene might offer some new insight.

Ashley was ready and waiting for him on the front steps of the house. The weather was turning stormy again, and he saw she was wearing jeans, sweater, a warm jacket and some new walking shoes. As he brought the police car to a stop, she stood up with a hint of weariness in her movements. He had to control an impulse to ask immediately what was the matter. He knew the wrong approach could spark fire in those dazzling blue eyes of hers. Easy does it, he told himself.

"I like a woman who doesn't keep me waiting," he offered with a smile as he opened the door for her. "Have you had lunch?"

She shook her head. "I'll get a sandwich on the ferry."

"Good, I'll join you." He closed her door, went around the car, and slid into the driver's seat. "How's the work going?" he asked as they headed down the cliff road.

"Slowly, I'm afraid. In addition to all the clothing, there's an amazing assortment of other collectibles. There's a wealth of false hair pieces in various styles, pompadours, chignons, and long, flowing tresses."

"And they're worth something?" Brad asked skeptically.

"They'll bring a good price. Museums that have vintage displays would snap them up in a minute for their mannequins. I can't even imagine what else I'll find when I open some of the wooden chests," she said in leaden tone.

He gave her a searching look. "The last time we talked, you were excited about doing the collection."

"I guess I'm tired, and a little strung out," she admitted.

"Care to tell me why?" he asked politely. With anyone else, he would have bluntly demanded to know what was the matter.

She looked out the window for a long minute before she turned in the seat to face him. "Something happened last night. And don't tell me I was seeing things!"

"All right, I won't," he said, raising an eyebrow slightly at her fiery command. "What did you see?"

"I'm not sure." She told him about chasing a fleeing figure through the house in the middle of the night. "I had the impression it was a woman in a white flowing dress."

"And you never caught up with it...her?"

She shook her head. "I felt a brush of cold air when she disappeared at the foot of some stairs. I thought that there must be an outside door there, but I couldn't find one."

"So it must have been someone who knew the house well."

Her expression was one of relief, as if she had been prepared for his making some doubtful response. "Aren't you going to tell me I was just seeing things the way I did on the widow's walk?"

"No, that could have been an illusion of light and shadows," he replied. "Obviously, your fleeing figure was not an illusion. Let's assume it was a woman who knew her way around the house. There aren't many possibilities. Ellen Brenden, Mrs. Mertz, Clara, and one part-time older kitchen maid."

"What about the guest house? I'm pretty sure I saw someone waiting for Fontaine when we arrived yesterday."

"Probably Clayton's night nurse, Linda Nigel." Even though the lawyer had been discreet, Brad knew Fontaine enjoyed more than a casual relationship with the nurse during his visits. "She comes at bedtime and leaves right after breakfast—most days." *Except when she hangs around to keep Fontaine company.*

"Oh, that's the way it is," Ashley said as if reading his thoughts.

"I don't see what Linda would have to gain by trying to scare you enough to have you leave." He frowned. "Of course, it could have been Ellen or the housekeeper for reasons of their own."

"Why would my staying and finishing the job matter to anyone?"

"If we knew that, we'd probably know who assaulted your sister," he answered grimly.

Ashley sighed. "Mrs. Mertz has been snooping around. When I came in the workroom and surprised her, she had some of the trunks and boxes open."

"Like she was looking for something specific?"

"I don't know. She claimed that Jonathan had asked her to keep on eye on things." After a minute, she added "I think Jonathan might have been going over the collection himself. A necklace that his late wife is wearing in a portrait is missing. There may be other personal mementos that he's removing without anyone noticing."

"It all ties together somehow." He gave her a reassuring smile, hoping to ease the frown on her face. "Piece by piece, we'll make sense of it."

When they reached the pier, he parked the police car. "Bill's out in the patrol boat. We'll use my car this afternoon on the mainland."

After buying sandwiches and drinks at the ferry's lunch counter, they sat on the open deck to eat. The wind was brisk and the water choppy. Neither one of them was very talkative, but the silence was a companionable one, and Brad was surprised how pleasant the routine crossing was in her company.

After leaving Ashley at the hospital, he drove about ten miles up the coast to a small resort where a retired police officer had a small home near the water.

Jim Mayberry was a rather stout man who wore comfortable overalls after years in a stiff uniform. He greeted Brad warmly and offered him a cold beer. As they sat on his small porch, they shared some mutual stories about law enforcement before Brad brought up the reason for his visit.

"There's been an assault on a young woman who was working at the Langdon compound while she organized an old collection of clothes and items for an auction house," he explained. "Since I've been unable to find any motivation in the current situation warranting such an attack, I've been wondering if the answer might lie in the past. The history of the Langdon family has some perplexing tragedies."

Jim nodded. "Well, there were plenty of questions about Samantha Langdon's accident and not too many answers. It was stormy as hell that night. Pea-soup fog and rain pouring down like it was coming from an open faucet. I was on night duty and had already been called out a half dozen times before the report came in on that accident. As it happened, somebody had seen her car lights miss a sharp curve and go off the road, or we wouldn't have known about it 'til daylight. Even then, it was too late to do anything. The car was almost entirely submerged, and divers had to bring her body up."

"She was alone, then?"

He took another deep swig of beer before answering. "Funny thing about that. We tried to backtrack her activities that night but came up empty. We know she drove her car out of the pier parking lot earlier that evening." Frowning, he stared at his nearly empty bottle. "That's all we knew—for sure."

"And what didn't you know for sure, Jim?"

"Whether or not she was alone." He stroked his bearded chin. "No other bodies surfaced, but..."

"But?" Brad prodded.

"The person who reported the accident said he had the impression there were two people in the car that night, but only one body surfaced—Samantha Langdon's. Visibility was so limited in the fog and rain that his statement was dismissed."

"Is it possible that there could have been someone with her? Someone who made it out of the car and disappeared before the rescue began?"

He nodded. "Twenty-five years ago, we didn't have the forensic capabilities we have today. I interviewed Samantha Langdon's personal maid, a young girl named Mary Sandrow who obviously idolized her mistress. I always felt she could have shed some light on who might have been with Samantha that night, but when it came to giving any information, she closed up tighter than a clam."

"Is she still around?"

"The last I heard Mary Sandrow was living on Minnequa Island. She quit the Langdons right after the funeral. Let's see, she'd be in her early forties about now."

"Maybe I'll pay her a visit."

Jim offered Brad another beer, but he shook his head. "Thanks a lot, Jim. Enjoy your retirement."

As he drove back to the hospital to pick up Ashley, his thoughts were centered on the possibility that Samantha Langdon might not have been driving her car when it went off the road. Was it possible some evidence remained in the vintage collection that was forcing the hand of someone who didn't want the truth to come to light?

ASHLEY COULD TELL Brad was preoccupied when he came into Lorrie's hospital room. His brow was furrowed, his expression tense; she wondered what had happened to make his thoughts so heavy.

Lorrie was sitting in a chair, sipping a lemonade. Ashley was delighted with her sister's quick recovery. They'd even taken a short walk down the hall to the visitors' lounge, and the doctors expected to release her in a day or two.

"That's great, Lorrie," Brad said when they told him the good news. "You're one tough cookie."

"Now I know what they mean by having a hard head," she said, laughing.

"I have a few more questions, Lorrie, if you don't mind answering them."

"I really haven't remembered anything more."

"That's all right," he assured her. "I'm just trying to fill in a little background. I was wondering if anyone in particular seemed especially interested in what you were doing in the workroom?"

"Gee, a lot of people kept popping in and out. When I first got there, Jonathan was the one who ordered worktables set up and made sure all the things in the attic were brought down. Clara helped me get the room organized and moved some things for me when I needed help."

"Anyone else?"

"Ellen was kind of a pest, wanting to handle everything and I had to stop her from unpacking some of the trunks. At mealtime, Langdon the elder would quiz me, mostly about the market value of the collection. Mr Fontaine seemed interested in the same thing. He stopped by just to chat a couple of times. I guess his firm handles the Langdon finances. He mentioned an investment they were considering. I didn't pay much attention."

"You never found anything missing?" Brad prodded.

Even as Lorrie shook her head, Ashley spoke up. "There was a necklace in an assortment of old jewelry that you photographed, Lorrie, but I couldn't find it when I made the inventory."

Ashley described the ornate locket necklace, and Lorrie shook her head. "It should have been with the other pieces if I logged it."

"I'm sure Samantha Langdon was wearing a necklace like it in a portrait Jonathan has in his study."

"Maybe he confiscated it for old times' sake," Lorrie suggested.

"That's what I thought," Ashley agreed. "I could tell Jonathan was hiding his emotions when he talked about his late wife."

Brad had remained silent during this exchange. Ashley wondered if he was weighing what they were saying as being significant or worthless.

When she asked him, he responded, "Everything in a criminal case is significant. I'm interested in anything connected with the Langdon household, past or present. All the pieces have to fit together somehow."

"You can't think the Langdons had anything to do with my attack," Lorrie protested. "I came to the island at their request. I was just doing my job."

"Maybe too well," he answered crisply.

THE WEATHER had improved during the afternoon, and by the time they docked back at the island's pier, a lowering sun was shining boldly through dissipating fog. Brad must have read her reluctance to return to the gloomy house and the tedious work awaiting her.

"There's more to the island than the Langdon compound," he said casually as they approached the parked police car. "Would you like to see the northeast section where I live? I'd like to show it to you. There's a nice little community of resident islanders along the shoreline."

The opportunity to spend some leisure time with him brought a surprising lift to her spirits.

Some of the houses hugging the rocky coast were weathered and bleached, such as the one where Bill

Hunskut lived with his widowed mother, others were quite modern, freshly painted white clapboard homes with well-kept yards.

"That's Dr. Hadley's place. And this is mine," Brad said as he turned the car into a short driveway beside a small, steep-roofed stone house facing the ocean. Clumps of grass edged a rock walk leading to the back door, and vegetation hugged the rock exterior. An enthusiastic young Labrador in a dog run dashed about, welcoming him home.

"That's Rusty," he told her. "The young pup was abandoned by a summer tourist last July." His voice softened in a way she hadn't heard before. "We kinda adopted each other."

She smiled as she watched him stoop down to accept the dog's leaping antics and enthusiastic, licking tongue.

"Okay, boy, that's enough. We've got company."

Laughing at his gyrating tail, Ashley patted the dog's head. "Nice to meet you, Rusty."

"He's ready for his evening walk." He raised a questioning eyebrow as he looked at Ashley.

"I'm game," she said.

"Good."

They took a steep path down to the water's edge, where huge boulders made deep caverns along the shoreline. As they walked along the edge of the ocean, Brad entertained her with stories of wrecked pirate ships and the treasures supposedly left behind in some of the underground caverns.

"When I was young, I searched all these caves for

pirate gold. I nearly got caught once by the incoming tide." He gave that deep, rumbling laugh of his. "My dad threatened to give me a tanning over that."

He talked about his mom and dad, and how he worked in the mercantile store until they sold it. By the time they had returned to his house, she realized Brad was no longer just a man dedicated to keeping the law on this misty island, but that it was part of the blood than ran through him. She knew if he ever married, it would have to be to a woman who could find fulfillment in a limited daily life on an island. *Goodness,* she thought, *why did I jump to that idea? I've just met the guy.*

They were both hungry and tired and she welcomed his suggestion that they drive back to the café and grab a bite to eat before he drove her back to the compound.

Brad pulled into his designated place at the pier when a young fisherman came running over to the car.

"You'd better come, chief," he said breathlessly. "There's a fight at Neptune Bar. Sloane's beating the hell out of some guy."

"Stay here," he told Ashley as he left the car. With a long stride he headed for the bar with the fisherman right on his heels.

As Ashley waited, she watched gray twilight bleach all color from the water. A few fishing boats anchored for the night, and a stillness settled on the empty wharf. As the minutes passed and the first spattering of stars dotted the darkening sky, Ashley grew restless.

She got out of the car and walked slowly along the water's edge for a short distance in the direction Brad had taken. The pub was set back in the trees, away from the shoreline. Even though she glimpsed lights and heard music, the building's isolation made her decide to turn around and go back to the car.

Before she had taken a dozen steps, she heard heavy breathing behind. She swung around. A disheveled man with blood on his face grabbed her. His eyes stared into hers with fiery hatred as he held a bloody knife inches from her neck.

"One squeak and I'll gut you like a fish. I know all about you and that sister of yours. Made up all kinds of lies, she did. Set the law on me!"

Sloane!

With the knife still at her throat, he forced her into the trees and down into a marshy gully. Rotting seaweed and rank-smelling water assaulted her nostrils. He threw her to the ground and bent over her with lusty fury.

Her hands clawed the rough ground beneath her as he laughed and pressed her shoulders to the wet ground. The sound of the nearby surf pounding against the granite boulders filled her ears with a deafening roar and drowned out her cries.

"No, no…" she cried as she struggled to get free.

He was laughing drunkenly at her resistance when her fingers found a loose, jagged stone in the wet marsh. The smile was still on his face when she struck him on the side of the head with all her force.

He cried out, stunned.

She scrambled to get away, clawing her way over the

jagged pile of rocks. He was after her in an instant, bellowing cuss words as he tried to grab her.

Her feet kept slipping in the soft slimy dirt and seaweed. He almost had her when suddenly he backed off. He turned to run away just an instant before Brad tackled him with a force that sent them both rolling on the ground. The half-drunk Sloane was no match for the pounding fists that landed squarely all over him. Brad cuffed him before the man could recover from the blow that had sent him sprawling on the soggy ground.

"Make another move and I'll break every blasted bone in your body."

She whimpered in relief as Brad put his arms around her trembling body. She was coated with mud and slime.

"Are you hurt? We'll get you to the doctor."

"No, I'm all right," she said in a shaky voice. "He didn't…I mean…nothing…nothing happened."

She saw the flood of relief in his tense face. "I would have killed the bastard. How'd you get away?"

"Hit him in the head, with a rock. It stunned him a little. If you hadn't come…" Her voice broke.

"But I did. And you can be damn sure he'll never bother you again." He glared down at the prone man as if he were ready to land a thick boot in the middle of Sloane's stomach.

Deputy Bill came running up to them, out of breath. "I came as soon as I got your page." His eyes widened as he took in Ashley's disheveled appearance and Sloane's drunken body sprawled on the ground. "What happened?"

"Sloane knifed a guy and then fled the saloon," Brad

answered grimly. "The drunken coward was hiding in these rocks when Ashley walked by. He dragged her down in the gully, but she hit him in the head with a rock and got away."

"Good girl," Bill said.

"While I'm locking Sloane up and writing up charges, I want you to drive her back to the Langdons'."

"Sure thing."

Brad brushed back tangled hair from Ashley's cheek. "Will you be alright?"

As he put his protective arm around her, she managed to nod. Her pride wouldn't let her admit that a lingering terror permeated every cell in her body.

Chapter Eight

When Ashley woke up the next morning, she couldn't believe she'd slept through the night without reliving the nightmare.

Deputy Bill had let her out at the front door of the house, and she'd made it up the stairs and to her room without anyone noticing. After stripping off her dirty, torn clothes, she'd filled the bathtub and let her raw-edged nerves mend as she soaked in the soothing warm waters. Emotionally and physically drained, she slipped into her pajamas and sat on the edge of the bed, staring at the floor for a long time.

An hour later, Clara brought up a dinner tray.

"Aren't you feeling well?" the maid asked, noticing Ashley was ready for bed.

"Just tired." Ashley knew her story would be all over the island soon enough, and she wasn't going to relive the horror by talking about it.

Hesitating at the door, Clara said, "I have a friend who cleans Dr. Hadley's house and she told me she saw you and the Officer Taylor walking his dog this afternoon." She gave Ashley a knowing smile. "I guess you wore yourself out with…exercise."

The implication that she and Brad had been intimate wasn't lost on Ashley, but at the moment she was too mentally and physically exhausted to worry about it. Let them think what they would. She didn't care, and she doubted very much that Brad would, either.

"I'll see to your soiled clothes," Clara said picking up the ones Ashley had piled in the bathroom. She wrinkled up her nose at the smell and looking questioningly at Ashley.

"I fell into a little puddle on the beach," she lied.

After the maid left, Ashley halfheartedly picked at the food on her tray. Then she set it aside, fluffed her pillow and turned on her side. Surprisingly, she fell into a deep sleep until morning.

She was dressed and ready to go downstairs for breakfast when there was a light knock on her door. Her eyes did a double take when she opened it and saw Dr. Hadley standing there.

"Good morning." The doctor greeted her as if this were a social visit even though he was carrying his medical kit. "Officer Taylor told me what happened. He asked me to stop by and make sure that you were all right."

"Oh, I'm fine, thank you," she answered quickly, surprised and pleased that Brad had sent him.

"That's good news. He'll be relieved, I know. Brad was pretty upset when I talked to him."

"I appreciate his concern, but I slept well and was just going to join the others for breakfast."

"Well, then, I'll walk down with you. How is your sister doing?" he asked politely as they made their way down the long hall.

"Very well. She's going to be released soon."

"I'm happy to hear that. I hope you are progressing nicely with your work. I trust that except for last night's unfortunate occurrence, you're enjoying your time on the island."

"Officer Taylor showed me around Pirates Point." she said, wondering if he'd seen them walking on the beach past his house. Apparently living in a goldfish bowl was part of daily life on Greystone. "The rocky shoreline is astounding."

"The island has its own special charm and Brad is certainly the man to convince you of that. We've been neighbors ever since he moved back to the island. Maybe you'll decide to give up city life and stick around for a while?"

"No chance of that," she answered firmly. "I'm a city girl with responsibilities. The sooner I get back to them, the better." She wasn't about to fuel the gossip pipeline with any romantic innuendos about her and the island's police chief.

"Well, there are always vacations."

"How's Mr. Langdon?" she asked, purposefully changing the subject.

"Clayton is holding his own against a variety of health issues. He's always been such an active man.

This forced retirement is hard on him." The doctor smiled at Ashley. "I think he would enjoy visiting with a pretty lady if you have the time."

"I suppose I could," Ashley answered without much enthusiasm.

"I just checked on him. He's had a good night. After breakfast might be a good time. His night nurse, Linda, goes off duty about then. Have you met her?"

"No, I haven't," she answered and silently added, *but I'd like too.* Brad had said the nurse was probably the one Ashley had glimpsed in Fontaine's guest cottage. "How do I find Mr. Langdon's rooms?"

"Just go down this hall, past the main staircase, turn to your right at a dissecting corridor which will eventually lead to the south wing of the house. Clayton's suite is behind the double doors at the very end."

The doctor left her at the door of the dining room, explaining that he'd had his breakfast earlier. Ellen Brenden and Fontaine were sitting at the table, engaged in a rather heated discussion of New York politics.

They barely nodded at Ashley as she poured her coffee and chose a warm muffin from the sideboard. Even though she hadn't eaten much last evening, her appetite was still suffering from the emotional drain of Sloane's assault.

Grateful that Dr. Hadley seemed to be the only one who had heard about the attack, she pretended to be interested in their debate, but excused herself before she'd had a second cup of coffee.

"Will we see you at lunch?" The lawyer seemed

surprised and a little annoyed at her quick departure. His face was flushed, as if the debate had riled him for some reason.

"Probably not," Ashley replied evenly and gave him a perfunctory smile. "Have a good day."

As she left the dining room, Ashley debated whether to visit the querulous old man or not, but her curiosity about Linda Nigel won out.

After mounting the main staircase, she turned in the opposite direction from her room. Several short corridors led off the hall to closed single doors; even with Dr. Hadley's directions, she almost missed the hall leading to the south wing of the house. A twinge of memory of having chased the fleeing figure down a similar hall tugged at her as she made her way to double carved doors at the end of a long corridor.

Her knock was rather bold and demanding, but it seemed like an eternity before a blond young woman in a white uniform opened the door. As she waited for Ashley to identify herself, her frank gaze assessed Ashley's new trim slacks and matching coral pullover. Her expression was questioning, but a glint in her steady eyes hinted that the nurse knew exactly who she was.

Ashley introduced herself in a businesslike tone. "I'm Ashley Davis. Dr. Hadley suggested that I visit Mr. Langdon. Is this a convenient time?"

"I'll see if Mr. Langdon is up to having a visitor." She stepped back and opened the door wider.

Ashley judged her to be no older than in her late twenties. She was attractive enough, but not pretty.

She certainly didn't act sophisticated enough to attract a middle-aged man like Fontaine. Leaving Ashley standing by the door, she crossed a spacious sitting room and disappeared into an adjoining bedroom. Ashley heard a murmur of voices and shortly the nurse came to the bedroom door and motioned to her. "Mr. Langdon will see you...but not for very long," she warned.

For some reason, Ashley had expected Clayton Langdon to be in bed, but he wasn't. He was sitting in a wheelchair parked near windows that offered a panoramic view of the western side of the island and the surrounding ocean waters. She suspected that during the day, the old man could watch fishing vessels come and go in the waters around the island.

His heavy-lidded eyes fixed on her as she approached him. His mouth sagged, his breath was short, and from his glaring expression she wondered if he had many visitors who weren't needing or demanding something from him. The nurse left them alone. From what Dr. Hadley had said, she was about to go off duty.

She hardly knew how to begin a conversation. She hadn't seen enough of him to pretend any kind of friendship. He would be doubly suspicious of someone pretending to be overly concerned about his health. The only thing they had in common was Lorrie. "I thought you might be interested to know that my sister will be leaving the hospital in a few days," she began smoothly. "She's made a wonderful recovery and will be going to California to spend some time with friends."

She expected him to make some conventional reply but he didn't. His scowl only deepened as he growled, "The Langdon curse." He clenched his purple-veined hands. "It's not easy on women."

"Curse?" she echoed softly as she eased down on a nearby chair.

"Took my granddaughter, it did." His tired eyes slid to a gold frame on a nearby table that held a photograph of a beautiful young girl laughing at the camera. He took it in his hands.

Because Ashley had been sleeping in his granddaughter's bed, looking into the same mirrors and bathing in the same tub, her skin suddenly prickled. In some strange way, she felt a kind of eerie kinship with the young woman who had lost her life, whether accidentally or by design.

"My poor Pamela." He stared at the photo as if he'd forgotten Ashley was there. When he suddenly turned and fixed his hypnotic eyes on her, she was startled by the sudden emotion in his voice. "The Langdon curse! Her mother, too. You know about Samantha?"

She was glad Brad had filled her in on the tragedy that had taken Samantha Langdon's life. "The car accident."

The old man leaned back in his chair and sighed heavily. "Not a good marriage. Jonathan should have married Ellen. Samantha was more suited to my younger son, Philip. Pamela might have escaped the curse if she'd had a different mother." Tears began to trickle down his wrinkled cheek.

Ashley sat there in silence. After a few minutes, the

nurse reappeared. As she took the photograph from his hand, she gave Ashley a dismissing nod. "Mr. Langdon needs to rest now."

Ashley stood up, not knowing what to say or do. When she reached out and squeezed Clayton's hand, he didn't respond.

The nurse followed her to the door.

"I don't know why Dr. Hadley wanted me to visit him," Ashley admitted.

"He was probably hoping your visit would take Mr. Langdon's mind off the past," she said in a tone that implied Ashley had put Pamela's picture in his hands. "What's done is done," she added rather sharply.

"Have you been with the family a long time, Miss Nigel?" Ashley asked in a tone she used for employees.

Obviously the nurse thought it was none of Ashley's damn business. She seemed to debate whether or not to answer. In a clipped voice, she said, "More than a year. I was recommended by Paul Fontaine. He's a *close* friend of mine."

Her meaning was not lost on Ashley. By *close,* she meant intimate. As the nurse closed the door, Ashley wondered if Linda Nigel was devoted enough to be involved in any schemes the New York lawyer might entertain?

Ashley retraced her steps to the second-floor main corridor and then headed toward the workroom. She needed to make up for yesterday's trip to the hospital and her time with Brad.

She stiffened when she saw the door to the workroom

was slightly open, and once again regretted being unable to lock it. She had no idea how much traffic went in and out of the room while she was away.

She braced herself to have another showdown with the housekeeper, but it was Ellen Brenden who was examining the contents of a large box. She looked startled when Ashley entered.

Giving a short laugh, she held up a large brimmed hat with dotted veil and peacock feathers dangling to one side. After setting it on her head, she put a finger under her chin in a coquettish pose. "Well, what do you think? High tea and crumpets this afternoon, dear?"

Ashley couldn't help but chuckle. There was something girlish and playful about the woman's behavior. The memory of Clayton saying, "Jonathan should have married Ellen," caused Ashley to wonder if the old man might have been right. Since Samantha had died when Pamela was just a baby, Jonathan could have married Ellen and provided a mother figure for his daughter all these years. Things might have turned out differently for Pamela if he had.

"Here, you try this one." Ellen reached into the box and brought out another fancy bonnet decorated with ribbons and flowers.

Ashley hated to spoil Ellen's fun but playing dress-up wasn't on her agenda. She shook her head. "I'm already behind on the inventory. I really have to finish up as quickly as I can and call the auction house for pickup."

Ellen sighed as she took off her bonnet. "Of course. I completely understand."

Ashley softened her tone. "I've been tempted to try on some of the gowns to see how I'd look."

"With your figure, you could handle a bustle and long train beautifully. I'd trip over my own feet. Once Samantha and I dressed up for a vintage ball in Boston. She was so beautiful," Ellen said with a sigh. "You can't imagine the collection of men always around her—single and married, young and old. It didn't matter." Her eyes were wistful as she confessed, "I couldn't help but be a little jealous."

"But you did marry?"

"Briefly, when I was nineteen years old. Kent is my ex-husband's nephew. He latched on to me a couple of years ago."

There was no need for her to elaborate. It was more than obvious that "Aunt Ellen" was a source of money and a valuable connection to people like the Langdons, who had plenty of it.

"I've been fortunate that Clayton and Jonathan have had a need for me all these years. I've never been able to take Samantha's place, of course, but I feel like part of the family."

"You're a valuable member, Ellen," Ashley assured her. "They're lucky to have you."

"That's what Dr. Hadley says." Her round face brightened. "He told me I would have made a good nurse. I sure know enough to tell when one of them isn't doing a good job."

"I just met Miss Nigel," Ashley commented purposefully. Ellen frowned but didn't rise to the bait.

Obviously, she was above gossiping about the hired help. "I came to see you because I wanted to apologize for this morning. It was terribly rude of Mr. Fontaine and myself to ignore you like that. Sometimes that man acts too big for his tailor-made britches and I can't keep my mouth shut. Just because he and Jonathan went to the same college doesn't mean he can be indiscreet when he visits here. He always has an eye out for a pretty girl."

Ashley stiffened. "Did he pay attention to Lorrie?"

"Fontaine pays attention to anything in a skirt," she said flatly and turned toward the door. Pausing, she looked back at Ashley. "Be careful."

The ominous tone of her words lingered in the room after she'd left. Ashley's thoughts kept scattering as she tried to turn her attention to the work at hand. *Why was Ellen warning her?* Ashley hadn't felt the lawyer's attention was anything but polite friendship. *Had Lorrie felt the same?* One thing was sure—she was going to tell Brad what Ellen had said. Maybe he could get some new insights from her.

IT WAS midmorning when the Portland police patrol boat arrived to pick up Sloane and take him to a lockup on the mainland. Brad was ready with the necessary papers for arrest and arraignment.

"Don't give him an inch of leeway," he warned as the two officers took the sour-faced, foul-mouthed prisoner into custody.

"I'll get you for this!" Sloane snarled, his eyes

bloodshot and his mouth twisted. "That high-and-mighty broad of yours better watch out. Next time will be a hell of a lot different."

"You got that right," Brad said icily. "Next time there won't be enough of you in one piece to haul away."

As the boat became a dot in the distance, Brad glanced at his watch. He wondered if Ashley would be making her daily visit at the hospital. He decided to stop by his house, grab a sandwich, let the dog out, and then make a quick run up to the compound to see if she needed a ride to the ferry.

As he passed the doctor's house, he saw Hadley heading toward the water with a fishing pole and basket. He escaped in his small boat as often as the demands for his service would permit. Unfortunately, that wasn't very often.

Braking quickly, Brad called out to him. "Wait up, Doc."

He turned around, frowning. Brad could tell he was expecting some kind of emergency to keep him from his afternoon escape.

Brad had spent a restless night worrying about Ashley and if he hadn't been tied up with Sloane, he'd have gone up there first thing himself. Concerned, he had called Hadley early the next morning to look in on her.

"Did you see Ashley?" Brad asked as he got out of the car.

"I did," he told Brad. "The lady said she appreciated your concern, but she was fine. From her appearance and manner, I would judge she was telling the truth."

The doctor smiled. "Of course, it wouldn't do any harm for you to ask her yourself, Brad."

"I think I'll do just that. I'll tell her it's doctor's orders."

"That might work," he said, chuckling as he turned away.

When Brad reached the Langdon house, he decided to go around to the family room entrance instead of knocking at the front door.

As he circled the house, he had a good view of the guest cottage a short distance below. No sign of the lawyer or anyone else on the premises. He made a mental note to have another chat with Linda Nigel. When he had questioned her the day of Lorrie's disappearance, she claimed she'd left the house after her night shift was over. He'd never been able to verify it.

When Brad entered the house through a side door, the only one in the family room was Ellen's nephew, Kent Brenden. The young man sat in a lounge chair holding a bottle of beer, with the remains of a sandwich on a plate beside him.

"Hi, Officer, join me for lunch?" he asked with a sociable smile.

"Just had mine," Brad replied.

"Too bad. I wouldn't mind the company."

"Where are the others?"

He shrugged. "Don't know. Aunt Ellen sent me in here to eat. Sometimes I think she'd like to keep me incognito, you know what I mean?"

"I think so. You don't quite fit in?" Brad asked in an encouraging tone.

"Neither does she!" he scoffed.

"Why do you say that?"

"All these years, Aunt Ellen's been hardly more than an unpaid servant. If Samantha hadn't had some stocks and bonds in her name and left them to Aunt Ellen, she wouldn't have enough money for a hot dog, but she has money." He scowled. "You'd think she'd be more generous with family."

"Meaning you, Kent?"

"Hell, yes. I'm the only family she's got. It ain't right I have to beg, borrow and—"

"Steal?" Brad finished for him.

Kent glared at him. "You can't prove I ever stole a dime."

Brad felt a movement behind him and turned around. Ellen stood just outside the family room door. How much she'd heard, he couldn't tell.

"I didn't know you were here, Officer." She had a fixed smile on her lips as she came in and greeted him. "You're a little late for lunch."

"I came to see Miss Davis."

"Oh, Ashley didn't come down for lunch. I think she's still working. Would you like me to show you the way?"

"I checked out the workroom after Lorrie's assault," he said, "but I'm not sure I could easily find it from this part of the house." He hoped the lie would give him a chance to speak with her in private.

Ellen turned to her nephew. "I'll be back in a few minutes, Kent." When they were out of the room, she said to Brad, "I hope you haven't gotten the wrong impression of my nephew. He's really a very nice young man. Just hasn't found himself. Reminds me of Timothy Templeton."

"Templeton?" Brad asked, pretending ignorance.

"You know, the young man Pamela was engaged to marry. He was too busy trying to live up to marrying a Langdon to really find himself. Kent's like that. He wants to ride the Langdon coattails to money and success." She pursed her lips as she added, "And there's very little of either to spread around."

Brad studied her expression and wondered if she was speaking for her nephew or for herself. Certainly her position in the family all these years was rather nebulous.

When they reached the workroom, it was obvious to Brad that Ashley was surprised to see him. Her eyes widened as she gave him a welcoming smile.

"Just checking up on you," he said lightly.

"Thanks."

Ellen studied them both for a moment, then mumbled something about Kent waiting for her and quickly made her exit. Since the woman hadn't mentioned the attack, Dr. Hadley had kept the incident to himself.

"I'm okay," Ashley quickly reassured him. "Didn't the doctor tell you?"

"Yes, but I wanted to see for myself," he said as he lightly cupped her chin and looked into her lovely blue eyes. Her breathing suddenly quickened as his finger-tips traced the sweet curve of her neck. He felt the magnetic draw of a desire between them. If she'd leaned toward him in the slightest, he would have kissed her, but in that tense moment of sexual attraction, he felt her defenses go up.

She turned away quickly and keeping her back to him, she fumbled with something on the worktable.

He stood there for a long moment, not knowing how to apologize for something he really didn't understand. He suddenly seemed to be a stranger to himself as he realized what had happened. For the first time in his life, he was falling hard and fast.

When he found his voice, he said huskily, "If you needed a lift to the ferry—"

"Oh I don't," she said quickly as she turned around. "I won't be going to the hospital today. Lorrie called and she's being released tomorrow morning. I'll go in on the early ferry and get her to the airport. She has a reservation for one o'clock. Our friends will meet her at the other end."

"That's great news. Well, then, would you like to take a run over to Minnequa Island with me in the patrol boat? It's a nearby island that's larger than Greystone and has shops, restaurants and tourist attractions. I need to talk to someone and thought a trip might take your mind off things."

"I'm tempted, but I really should stay and get this finished up as quickly as possible. If I work most of the day, I should be able to get almost everything packed."

"My appointment isn't until five-thirty," he added quickly. "It only takes about twenty minutes to cross the bay to Minnequa Island, so you'd still have most of the day to work. I could pick you up a little before five." As he saw signs of debate going on in her mind, he added, "We can make up for the dinner we missed last night."

"All right," she said finally and then added with a slight smile, "You do owe me a dinner."

"That I do," he agreed.

"Thanks for coming," she said softly as he turned toward the door.

"We'll make up for last night," he promised with all the confidence of someone brash enough to think negative forces were under his control.

Chapter Nine

Minnequa Island was a flurry of activity as Brad docked the patrol boat. A white-crested rolling surf rose and fell against a stone jetty, and a rising wind whipped breakers in the incoming tide. The wharf was crowded with returning fishermen hauling their catches to various fish houses. A nearby business district was alive with late shoppers and early patrons of the cafés and restaurants.

Brad pointed to some nearby houses north of the harbor. "I'm going to interview a Mary Sandrow who lives over there. She worked as a personal maid to Samantha Langdon until the car accident."

"And?" Ashley prodded, obviously curious.

"It's possible that after all these years she may be ready to talk. Who knows, she may have information that is pertinent in finding out who attacked your sister."

"I don't see how something that happened over twenty-five years ago could have anything to do with an assault on Lorrie, but you're the detective. The investigation is your call."

"I don't want to pass up any leads. I shouldn't be very long. Why don't I meet you at the Dolphin Inn in about an hour? They have good food and we can have our dinner without interruption."

"Promise?" she asked in a way that challenged his ability to keep the evening strictly impersonal.

"Would I lie?" he asked in mock indignation.

"Maybe." She gave him a knowing smile as she left him with a wave of her hand.

As she walked away, he felt a heat surging through him that was anything but indifferent to her sexual appeal. Her sensual walk, those long legs, supple hips and—

Whoa! he silently told himself and jerked his eyes away from her retreating figure. Until now, he'd managed to keep any romantic relationships on the light side. The truth was, he'd never met an independent, engaging woman like Ashley.

He'd only dated casually during his years on the mainland and since returning to the island, he'd stayed clear of female visitors who seemed ready to give him an inviting smile as he passed by. He certainly had more sense than to let down his guard and allow a California businesswoman play havoc with his emotions. *Didn't he?*

He jerked his mind back to business and headed toward Mary Sandrow's house. The attractive Cape Cod-style home was painted gray and had a picket fence around a small, fading flower garden. A tabby cat sat sunning itself on the front step as Brad let himself through a gate and approached the front door.

The woman must have been watching for his

approach because she opened the door before he had even raised his hand to knock. Brad gave her his best disarming smile, but it did little to soften the scowl on her pudgy face.

"I'm Officer Taylor—"

"I know who you are," she responded coldly. She was a large woman, overweight, with sagging jowls and cheeks that destroyed any hint of the attractive woman she might have been. Now in her forties, Brad had a difficult time picturing her as the personal maid Samantha Langdon had trusted with all her secrets.

"Thank you so much for seeing me," he responded politely, ignoring the hostility that radiated from her.

"What do you want? Why are you here?"

"Just to have a little talk with you."

"About what?"

"As I told you on the phone, I'm doing a little investigation into Samantha Langdon's death."

"What for? She's been long gone."

Brad reached out and opened the screen door between them. He sensed she'd fully intended to slam the door in his face but now it was too late.

"Do you mind if I come in?" The question was rhetorical. He'd already stepped across the threshold.

Scowling, she turned away from the door and waddled down a hall to a spacious room spanning the entire back of the house.

Much to Brad's surprise, the furniture and décor was very modern and quite new. Large windows were framed in rich fabric, and colorful imported rugs graced the hardwood floor. Everything was a sharp contrast to the rather disheveled appearance of Mary Sandrow herself.

He remained standing until she had eased down in a large overstuffed chair that could bear her weight without sagging. There was no pretense of a gracious hostess about her. She glared at him as he sat down on a sofa facing her. Her narrowed eyes never left his face. Everything about her posture gave the impression of a guard dog ready to spring.

"I'm here because you were closer to Samantha Langdon than anyone else at the time of her death." Brad had decided his best bet was to be completely honest with her. "I need some answers."

"Why?"

"Because I'm investigating an assault on someone working for the Langdons."

"I heard about that. Some city girl, wasn't she?" Her voice was flat, disinterested.

"Yes. Lorrie Davis. She was cataloging clothing and other things collected by the Langdon family through the years."

The woman shrugged. "The attic was jammed full of stuff when I was there. Never knew why they kept all of it. Someone was always talking about cleaning it all out, but no one ever did."

"I guess they never thought it was worth much—until now." Brad kept his voice level. "Do you know any reason, Mary, why going through any of Samantha's belongings might trigger some unexpected violence?"

She gave an ugly laugh. "You really are grasping at straws, aren't you?"

"Maybe so, but there are some things about Samantha Langdon's death that have me puzzled."

"My Samantha's dead, and that's that!" A sudden anguish laced her angry protest.

"You really loved her, didn't you? I don't expect there was anyone in the whole household who knew her as well as you did. She must have confided in you about everything."

He waited for the woman to deny it. When she didn't, Brad moved in quickly. "We have reason to believe Samantha Langdon wasn't alone that night when her car plunged off the road."

Mary Sandrow's face suddenly had a frightened expression of someone being cornered. She snapped, "I don't know anything about that night."

"What was she doing on the mainland?" Brad asked as if he hadn't heard her denial. "Was she meeting someone?"

"She…she was alone…the police said so."

"Let's see, how old were you when you started working at the compound, Mary? Barely eighteen, I believe. Just a few years younger than Samantha. You were her personal maid before and after she was married. When she died so tragically, you left the Langdon household. What did you do then?"

She glared at him, her mouth clamped shut.

"I know you moved to Minnequa Island, but there aren't any records of your being employed anywhere. Strange. Uncle Sam is quite a steward when it comes to keeping track of things like that. You've never filed any kind of reported income."

"I don't owe the government anything," she snapped.

"No, not if you haven't been gainfully employed all these years." As he looked around at the room's plush new furnishings, he said, "I can't help wondering how can you afford all this."

"Why don't you check my bank account?" she snapped.

"As a matter of fact, I have. The thirtieth of every month you make a sizable deposit—in cash."

"No law against putting money in a bank."

"That depends, Mary. What are you doing to get it?"

"Not a damn thing, Officer. Not a damn thing."

"Nothing?"

"Nothing!"

Brad's gut feeling was that she was telling the truth.

Someone had been paying Mary Sandrow all these years—and was still paying her just to keep quiet.

ASHLEY WAS ENJOYING the view and the fanciful undersea decor of the Dolphin Inn. Some of her built-up tension had begun to ease as she sat on a veranda and sipped a glass of wine. Lorrie would be leaving in the morning, and Ashley would be joining her in California before long. All that had happened to them here would seem like a strange dream.

Quickly forgotten?

When she saw Brad's easy gait making his way around the tables towards her, she knew some memories would last a lifetime. How could she forget the first time she'd seen him on the night of her arrival and the way he had bawled her out? In his jeans and pullover, she'd taken him for some officious deckhand.

"What are you smiling about?" he asked as he eased down into the chair opposite her.

"I was just thinking about how official you look in your uniform with your badge boldly displayed on your chest. Kind of intimidating."

With a quick movement, he removed the badge and stuck it in his breast pocket. "That better?"

"Much," she said. "More appropriate for a dinner date."

"Oh, is that what this is?" he teased.

Their light mood continued through dinner. Both of them needed a respite from talking about anything that really mattered as they discussed sports, movies, and hobbies. As they left the restaurant, Brad took her arm and turned her in the opposite direction of the wharf.

"Where are we going?" she asked, puzzled.

"I feel like dancing."

"What?" she echoed in disbelief.

"Dancing. You know, step, step, step together, step."

"Yes, but—"

"You think I can't put one foot in front of the other, is that it? I'll have to show you my trophy."

"Trophy?"

She thought he was pulling her leg until he explained that he and one of the female police cadets had entered a dance contest and won third place while they were at the academy.

"We would have come in first, but my partner wasn't that good." He grinned, obviously lying.

A community dance hall was filled with local people and others who had come from surrounding islands to enjoy Minnequa's nightlife. A five-piece band filled the barnlike structure with music. The main floor and a balcony crowded with tables offered food and drink.

"Shall we get a table later?" he asked. "Enjoy a few dances first?"

Even as she agreed, she wondered exactly what she was letting herself in for. How much should she believe about his agility on the dance floor? His tall, solid physique looked more akin to body-building activities than light-footed maneuvers on a dance floor. She hoped he wasn't going to embarrass himself and her.

The fast-paced, two-step tune wasn't what she would have chosen for their first sojourn onto the dance floor, but he easily swung her out in front of him, and then pulled her into dance position.

She'd never been so thankful for her five-foot, eight-inch height. She could look into his eyes and accommodate his six-foot frame to hers.

He hadn't lied.

As the energetic musicians struck up a lively measure, he displayed a natural rhythm and harmony with the music. They spun, parted, dipped and twirled around the floor. He led with a confident ease that made her a better dancing partner than she really was.

When the drummer put a defining beat to the last

note, she was out of breath and laughing. "Don't expect me to keep up this pace all evening."

She hoped the next offering might be a slow one, but it wasn't. As the music started, someone grabbed her free hand and pulled her and Brad into a group formation. Almost instantly, she found herself whirling away with a perfect stranger.

The tempo and sound kept getting faster and louder as she was twirled from one grinning partner to another. She made a full circle of the room before she dizzily found herself holding Brad's hands again.

"Thank heavens," she breathed in relief when the music stopped. The room was spinning like a top, and she clung to him to keep her balance.

"How'd you like that?" he asked, chuckling as he led her off the floor to one of the small side tables.

She groaned as she dropped into a chair. "Is that the way you islanders kill off the tourists?"

"Don't tell me a city gal like you can't dance the night away," he chided.

"That wasn't dancing," she protested.

"It's called the Island Whirligig. Not everyone can last until the final spin. You did well!"

They ordered a couple of drinks, talked and laughed, and watched the crowd circulating around them. When the lights dimmed for some romantic tunes, Ashley expected they'd return to the dance floor.

She hummed a familiar ballad and was ready to get to her feet when she realized Brad seemed to be ignoring the dance floor. He made small talk and sipped his beer.

She was surprised and disappointed when he made no move to ask her to dance again.

He glanced at his watch. "I guess we'd better head back. It's getting late."

Late? Late for what? Neither of them had a curfew.

"What's the matter?" she asked pointedly. "Did I embarrass you with my dancing?"

"No, of course not. It's just that this wasn't a good idea, after all." He reached across the table and took her hand. "I confess I'm a coward when it come to matters of the heart. I don't like dead ends. If things were different and you could stay…"

She shook her head. "I have a life waiting for me."

"Is there someone else?"

"No, not anymore. The man I thought I loved found someone else. Right now, I'm totally happy to be single." She finished the rest of her wine. "You're right. We really should be going. Lorrie will be leaving tomorrow, and I should be able to finalize everything in quick order."

THEY LEFT the dance hall and walked the short block to the wharf where the patrol boat was docked at the end of a long pier. Brad couldn't decide whether to thank her for the evening or leave well enough alone.

All through dinner, her appealing sexuality had quickened his desire. He'd suggested going dancing as an excuse to hold her close and torture himself with the brush of her body against his. But when the opportunity finally presented itself, he had pulled back. He'd never been one to lie to himself. It wasn't dancing he wanted. Ashley Davis fired him with desires that were full of red flags. He'd be a fool not to keep a tight rein on those feelings when he was with her.

He helped her aboard the boat and expected her to take the companion seat beside him, but she didn't. She went into the boat's cabin and sat down on one of the benches. Apparently she'd interpreted his behavior as motivation to put some distance between them.

He debated whether to let the whole thing pass. How could he admit that holding her in his arms, feeling her body pressed against his while they moved together to the seductive music, was too much of a challenge? He couldn't admit the truth without embarrassing them both, but his conscience prickled enough for him to try to salvage the evening.

"It's much nicer on deck. For once, we have a clear night. Why don't you—" He broke off as he noticed a faint, almost imperceptible glow under the door of a storage cabinet just beyond where she was sitting. "What the hell?"

In two long strides, he reached the cabinet and jerked open the door. An explosive device connected to some wires contained a faintly glowing timer, and only a few seconds were left in the countdown.

"Get off the boat," he yelled at her. "Now!"

She jerked to her feet as he knelt down and carefully lifted up the whole device.

Ashley ran ahead of him as he held the firebomb in his hands as steadily as he could and walked across the cabin. Holding his breath, he carefully mounted a step and crossed the deck to the railing. In slow motion, he leaned out as far as he could and dropped it. The last second ticked as dark, swirling waters sucked the firebomb out of sight.

Chapter Ten

"Run! There may be another one!" Brad grabbed Ashley's arm. They ran the length of the long pier before they stopped and looked back.

"What was it?" she gasped. She'd leaped off the boat just as Brad bent over the railing and dropped something into the water.

"A firebomb. Damn it! It couldn't have been there long! Somebody must have seen us leave the dance."

Ashley's legs were suddenly weak from fear and the horror of what might have happened. Trying to escape a burning boat miles from shore could have been deadly. Only Brad's strong grip kept her on her feet. He pulled her with him as they ran to a nearby emergency box on a pole a short distance away.

"Officer Taylor from Greystone Island," he barked into it. "Someone tried to torch my police cruiser at the pier. Couldn't have set it more than minutes ago. Yes. Right now!"

He hung up and turned to Ashley. "The police chief

is on his way. Go back to the restaurant. Stay around people until I come to get you." Then he added quickly as a kind of reassurance, "It's me they're after."

"But why?"

"I have a pretty good idea," he added grimly but didn't elaborate. Giving her shoulders a light push, he said, "Now go. I'll keep my eye on you until you're inside the restaurant."

In less than five minutes, Minnequa Police Chief Al Hubbord and one of his deputies arrived. The three men made a quick search of the cruiser, but no other incendiary device was found.

"We're not dealing with a professional firebug, that's for sure," Chief Hubbord commented. "But a jerry-rigged device can be just as deadly. Good thing you weren't halfway to Greystone when it ignited." He shoved a pair of glasses back on his large nose. "Got any idea who might have wanted to toast your cookies?"

"Several ideas," Brad admitted, "but no proof—yet."

Hubbord smiled. "I like the set of your jaw, Taylor. Let us know if we can do some legwork for you. My deputy dusted the cabinet for fingerprints and we'll let you know if we got any clean ones that don't belong to you or Deputy Hunskut."

Brad replied, "We use the boat to transport prisoners to the mainland. Identifying all the fingerprints may be a challenge."

Brad thanked him and watched them drive off. He knew there were a dozen places along the eastern coastline of Minnequa Island where a boat could anchor within walking distance of the long pier where the cruiser had been docked. Even at night, there was a lot of activity along the shoreline. He knew a search for any craft that might look familiar was a long shot. If someone had followed them from Greystone and planted the firebomb, he was pretty sure he'd recognize the boat. He strode a half mile in each direction without any luck

When he finally entered the restaurant, Ashley was sitting at a table near the windows. She must have seen him coming because her eyes were fixed on the doorway with a questioning look on her face.

As he slid into a chair opposite hers, she asked in an anxious voice, "What happened?"

"We checked out the cruiser. It's clean. Only one device. I doubt if fingerprints will turn up anything, but we'll see." She waited for him to continue but there were too many loose threads to be connected before he was willing to share them with anyone.

"So that's it," he said shortly. "If you're ready, we'll head back."

She opened her mouth and then closed it, as if she realized he was keeping his silence for some good reason.

He took her hand as they walked slowly down the pier to the police cruiser. He was grateful she didn't pelt him with a lot of questions he couldn't answer. He'd never known a woman who could act so bravely in such a circumstance. More and more, his feelings for her were threatening to spin out of control. He never begged a woman for anything, but he'd be willing to do it if he thought there was a chance she'd remain on the island with him.

She stood beside him as he started the engine and maneuvered the cruiser out into the open water. A whiteness in her face and a tightness around her mouth betrayed that she was half expecting the deck under her to suddenly explode into flames.

A protective surge made his voice husky as he reassured her quickly, "It's safe, sweetheart."

Sweetheart! The endearment startled him the instant it left his lips. He wasn't in the habit of using that kind of familiarity with women. If she was equally surprised, she didn't show it and stood closely beside him all the way back to Greystone.

After picking up the patrol car at the wharf and driving back to the Langdon compound, he saw her safely inside. "I'm terribly sorry," he said softly. "I should have known better than to mix business with pleasure. No need for you to be dragged into something that happened years ago. Honestly, I never expected the woman I went to see would sound an alert that her secret was in jeopardy."

"What secret?"

Instead of answering, he lightly brushed back wisps of hair trailing down on her forehead. The smooth touch of her skin and the warmth of her nearness as she lifted her face destroyed all his resolutions. He lowered his head and kissed her with a commanding possession that betrayed the intensity of his feelings. As his quickening tongue parted her lips, his hands splayed over her back, drawing her into the spiraling heat of his desire. She surrendered to his embrace and kisses with returned passion until he whispered, "You can't leave."

She turned her face away from his questing lips. As she pulled back from his embrace, she said, "This isn't good for either of us."

He started to argue, but common sense overrode his emotions. The events of the evening had left them both vulnerable, and in a way he was glad she had the sense to know it.

LATER THAT NIGHT, as Ashley lay wide awake staring at the ceiling of her bedroom, she wondered if the passion they'd felt was only a temporary release from a horror too real to handle alone. Understandably, the horrifying death threat had caused them to function at a high emotional pitch.

When she finally fell into restless sleep, subconscious fragments formed in dreamlike sequences. A threatening presence pursued her as she ran through a dense fog. When clawlike hands reached out of the mist and grabbed her, she cried aloud and jerked awake. She sat up, a pounding heartbeat in her ears and cold sweat covering her body.

Throwing back the covers, she went into the bathroom and bathed her face in cold water. As she stood looking in the mirror, her reflection made her a stranger to herself. Her eyes reflected a vulnerability she hadn't seen before. It was as if the hard shell of knowing exactly who she was and what she wanted out of life had somehow been damaged. She was falling in love, but would she make the biggest mistake of her life if she stayed on Greystone Island? A weird feeling was growing that the foggy island hated her. As she straightened her shoulders, she dismissed the impression as an understandable reaction to the unusual events that had engulfed her.

She glanced at her watch—nearly three-thirty. She needed to be at the hospital early enough to get Lorrie to the airport, but she doubted if she could readily get back to sleep.

"I might as well make use of the time by working on the inventory."

Putting on a robe over her pajamas, she crossed the hall to the workroom. She'd just turned on the light and sat down at the makeshift desk when Nurse Nigel appeared in the doorway. She was in her nurse's uniform, and a stethoscope hung around her neck.

The nurse's face was flushed and her hands clenched tightly at her sides. "What in the hell do you think you're doing? Playing some kind of sick game?"

"I don't know what you're talking about," Ashley answered just as forcibly.

"Don't pretend with me! Luckily Clayton was asleep when you did your macabre dance through the suite or he might have died in shock."

Ashley swallowed hard in astonishment.

"You didn't think I'd catch on, did you?"

"I don't know what—"

"You had me going for a while but it won't work,"

she declared angrily. "You thought I'd be too spooked to figure it out."

"Spooked?"

"Floating around in one of these old dresses. Making like a ghost." She gave a derisive laugh.

Ashley began to make sense of her tirade.

"It'll take more than that to scare me off," the nurse said as she walked over to a rack of hanging dresses. "Which one did you wear tonight? And where's the blond wig?"

"It wasn't me," Ashley replied calmly.

"Save your lying breath!"

"I know what you saw and it wasn't me."

"Who in the hell was it? A ghost?" The nurse gave a derisive laugh. "Spare me the crock of lies, please. I don't know what you and your sister's game is, but it won't work."

Ashley responded as evenly as she could, "You are jumping to the wrong conclusion—"

"You just happen to be up at three o'clock in the morning."

"I couldn't sleep. I decided to work."

"Really? It looks to me as if you just changed clothes. Did someone hire you to spook Clayton and give him a heart attack?"

Ashley got to her feet. "I know what you saw and I know you're looking for an answer. The truth is, I've been searching for one myself."

"Oh, really?" Her tone was mocking.

"A couple of nights ago I chased a fleeing figure

through the house. I never got close enough to determine who it might be," Ashley admitted and added, "The thought did occur to me that it could be you as well as anyone."

"Me? Don't be ridiculous." The nurse seemed to be indignant to find herself in the role of the accused. "Why in God's name would I do something so bizarre?"

"It's just possible you're trying to put the spotlight on me to cover up your own deceit."

"And what deceit might that be?" she scoffed.

"I don't know. Maybe your lover put you up to it? Paul Fontaine is your lover, isn't he?"

"That's none of your blasted business."

"Maybe it is," Ashley replied thoughtfully. "Especially if the two of you have some kind of hidden agenda."

"You and your sister are the ones playing dangerous games." Her tone was frigid. "You may not be as lucky as she was if you don't mind your own business." She threw out the warning like a live grenade, then turned and slammed the door behind her.

Ashley sat back down in the chair and stared at nothing for a long time. Then she let her eyes rove over the collection of garments hanging on racks or still sitting in open trunks. Boxes of hats and wigs remained to be inventoried. She'd been careful about unpacking more things than she could photograph, inventory, and box for shipping.

Anyone could have been removing complete outfits without her knowing it.

More than ever, she needed to get everything sent to

the auction house as soon as possible. Taking a deep breath, she set to work with a renewed determination.

A few hours later, the rising sun warned her she'd better get herself ready to catch the ferry.

BRAD WAS already at the office at sunrise, pondering some unanswered questions involving Mary Sandrow. As far as he knew, no one else had shown any interest in Samantha Langdon's old personal maid. She had only come to his attention because of his conviction that past Langdon tragedies might somehow be related. He'd been as surprised as anyone to discover that someone had been giving her cash to deposit into her bank account for a good many years. Why? If Mary was a blackmailer, why had she been safe from harm all these years and not silenced?

When he contacted her and set up a time to see her, she might have gotten scared and contacted someone who set the fire device on the cruiser in order to put a stop to his inquiry. He decided to ask Chief Hubbord to put a temporary surveillance on Mary Sandrow's house and see who might turn up.

He glanced at his watch and swore. Damn. He knew that Ashley was catching the early ferry to the mainland, and he planned to give her a ride to the wharf.

He hurried out of the office and was about to get into the police car when he stopped short. There she was! Heading for the dock's waiting area.

"You're early," he said as he caught up with her.

She looked a little surprised and startled. "A little, I guess."

"I'm sorry I didn't arrange to give you a ride down this morning."

"No problem. I needed the walk…to clear my head."

"I didn't sleep very well myself," he admitted. "I'm sorry if I was out of line last night. You have to believe, I didn't intend to come on that strong but—"

"It's not that," she cut in quickly, obviously not wanting to talk about the heated hunger between them. "It's something else. I had an early morning visit from Nurse Nigel."

"Is it Clayton?" he asked quickly.

She shook her head. "No, not at all. Something else entirely."

He listened as Ashley related the weird accusations the nurse had made. "She implied suspicion of Lorrie as well?"

Ashley nodded. "She asked who was paying us to scare Clayton enough to give him a heart attack. I accused her of having a hidden agenda for doing the dirty deed for herself and Paul Fontaine."

Brad gave a low whistle. "Well, that should have stirred things up a bit. I guess I'd better get myself up there while you're gone and look into it."

The ferry sounded a warning for loading. Brad reached into his pocket and drew out keys to his personal car. He put them in her hand. "Drive mine today. It'll be easier all around, getting to the hospital and airport. Don't argue," he said quickly as she opened her mouth to protest.

He knew he'd made a mistake when he impulsively

leaned over and kissed her lightly. Instantly, the warmth of her soft mouth invited a lot more than a lingering touch.

The ferry whistle sounded again.

He slowly released her and both of them stood there looking at each other as if there were more to say but neither of them could find the words.

"I'll meet the ferry this afternoon," he promised. "And fix dinner."

ASHLEY QUICKLY FOUND his car in the mainland's ferry parking lot. She eased into the driver's seat and sat there for a long moment, remembering how his large hands laid on the steering wheel and how his manly frame had filled the seat beside her. Even now the scent of his aftershave seemed to linger in the air.

She knew that if he'd been sitting beside her now, she would have welcomed his kisses and caresses. Did she really want to put herself through such an emotional wringer? Hadn't she learned enough in the past by opening her heart up to someone? She'd be gone in a few days. And then what?

Lorrie was ready and waiting for her when she reached the hospital. Ashley gave her a hug and said, "You look ready to enjoy the California sunshine."

"I called Ted and Amy this morning. They'll meet the plane."

"Are you sure you feel up to making the trip?"

"It's a direct flight, and I'll probably sleep most of the way."

To Ashley's relief, Lorrie chatted like her old self as

they drove to the airport. Her sister didn't seem to be particularly anxious about how the investigation was going, and Ashley avoided mentioning anything such as the attempt to set fire to the police boat. It was only when they were about to part at the airport gate that Ashley said she was going to have dinner with Officer Taylor.

Lorrie searched her face. "What is it, Ashley? You get a funny look when you mention his name. Don't tell me you've fallen for that big hunk of masculinity?"

Unable to summon up a lighthearted denial, she answered honestly, "I don't know, Sis."

"You can't be serious. Honey, you're not the love-'em-and-leave-'em type."

"I know it's crazy."

"You got that right! You're a smart businesswoman with a future. Don't get yourself into something that's got no chance of 'happily ever after'." Lorrie shook a warning finger at her. "You deserve something better. You weren't cut out to be somebody's little homemaker. Don't fool yourself."

Her sister's warning stayed with Ashley as she drove back to the wharf and parked Brad's car. With time on her hands before the afternoon ferry departed, she walked a few blocks to the downtown district where colorful shops and inviting boutiques drew her inside. She talked to some of the owners about her line of beaded purses and accessories and left her card with promises of sending a brochure of her latest catalog.

Ashley's mind was filled with these possible new accounts as she returned to the wharf. Lorrie was right.

For the first time since she arrived at Greystone, Ashley realized how much the life she'd made for herself meant to her. Becoming emotionally involved with any man who would expect her to give it up was out of the question. Still, there was no harm in enjoying his company for the next few days.

Brad was waiting for her when the ferry docked, and her determination to keep her emotions on an even keel was sabotaged from the very beginning. The way his dark eyes lit up when he saw her and the brush of his body against hers as they walked away from the pier sent all kinds of unbidden messages.

As they drove to his place, she indulged in a nervous babble about the prospect of gaining some new accounts along the mainland waterfront. She had never talked to him about her business, and once she started she couldn't seem to stop.

"My California outlets may be just the beginning. With time, I ought to be able to find markets nationwide, and maybe even overseas."

He listened politely, nodding and smiling. "Sounds as if you know where you want to go, alright. That's half the battle, isn't it?"

The way he said it brought her up short. She wanted to ask him what he meant, but the set lines in his face stopped her.

"Did you have a good day?" she asked, changing the subject.

"Nothing new. I'm doing some background checks on some possible leads." He gave her a wry smile. "Can we put the investigation aside for a few hours and pretend I'm just hosting a successful businesswoman for the evening?"

"Perfect," she agreed.

He let Rusty out and the dog bounded joyfully around their heels as they walked into the house through the back door. The kitchen was small, with ugly brown cupboards. No curtains hung at the half window and the only art on the mud-colored walls was a serviceable calendar. A plain set of salt and pepper shakers sat on the bare eating table.

The adjoining front room was equally stark. Furniture resembling bargains offered at secondhand stores indicated Brad's indifference to style and harmony. The complete lack of color and decoration assaulted Ashley's aesthetic senses. Color, texture, and design were such a part of her existence that once again she felt a stab of disappointment that they had so little in common. How could she live with a man who was blind to the sensual pleasures that were so important to her?

The only redeeming feature of the living room was a large picture window overlooking the ocean. He'd set a table outside on a small patio. A lovely view of the ocean made up for the stark interior of the house.

He poured them each a glass of burgundy wine and then sat down, stretching his long legs out in front of him in a languid way that made her more conscious than ever of his masculinity.

"You're not a vegetarian, are you?" he asked. "I thought I'd fix us a couple of porterhouse steaks."

"Sounds good."

As they sipped their wine, he asked, "Do you miss the city all that much?"

"Not at the moment," she admitted. "But I don't think I'd appreciate a steady diet of wind, water and fog for very long. I grew up in New York City and there's an addictive energy about crowds, noise and the ever-changing scenes." She had to make him understand. "I guess you either like it or you don't."

"I never did enjoy living on the mainland," he admitted. "Police work is demanding anywhere, but especially in the city. I could hardly wait to get back to Greystone."

"I've lived on both coasts and wouldn't mind trying Seattle or Chicago. If my business expands the way I hope, I'll probably rack up a fortune in frequent-flier miles."

"I'd bet you'll reach any goal you set. I don't think you'll get sidetracked." He got to his feet. "Well, I guess I'd better put on those steaks."

"Do you need some help?"

"No, just enjoy the peace and quiet, and take some of it back to California with you." There was a kind of dismissal in what he was saying.

He disappeared into the house and Ashley sank back in her chair, wondering why tears were close. She tried to remember why she'd felt so pleased about the possibility she'd found some new business outlets. All of that seemed hollow now.

What are you going to do about it?

The answer seemed simple. She wouldn't think beyond the few days that were left.

He brought out full plates of steak, corn and sliced tomatoes. He seemed a little surprised when she ate heartily and murmured, "Delicious."

"Would you like seconds?" he asked as he eyed her nearly empty plate. "There's only blueberries and cream for dessert…with coffee."

"Perfect. I love blueberries."

"Really? It's too bad you're not here during the picking season."

He shared stories with her about berry-hunting trips on the island. She could picture him as a gangling youngster darting about, trying to fill his pail before any of the others did. "The island has a lot to offer a young boy," he told her.

His brown eyes softened when he reminisced about his first homemade boat that came apart on its maiden voyage.

"My career as a seafaring adventurer was short-lived, but I've always loved the water. Would you like to see my favorite place in all the world?"

When she nodded, he stood up and held out his hand. His long legs easily mounted the piles of tumbled rocks along the rugged shoreline, and she fought a sense of vertigo as they climbed to a pinnacle of granite boulders that overlooked a sheer drop to the sea below.

"Now that's a view," he said proudly.

A terrifying one, she thought as she tried to smile in agreement.

"Have a seat."

Cautiously, she eased down on the rock slab beside him. Layers of huge granite slabs descended abruptly down to the water's edge, and she tried not to focus on the rolling breakers assaulting the sheer drop below.

"I climb up here when I need to get my head together about something…or someone." He glanced at her as if she might be included in the latter category. "What do you think?"

She put her hands flat down on the rock to make sure it wasn't sliding out from under her.

"Impressive," she managed to say.

"You're looking a little pale." He put his arm around her waist. "Don't you like heights?"

"I can take the Empire State Building in my stride," she answered a little defensively.

He chuckled. "I'm not sure I could. Frankly, I've never had the urge to see New York from that perspective. This is more to my liking. I've come out here at dawn, midday, twilight and midnight. It's my private sanctuary." He paused. "I've never brought anyone here before. Why do you think that is?"

"I don't know," she answered, too quickly. Was he exploring? Wanting some kind of commitment from her? If so, she had none to give.

He obviously wanted to share the rich natural treasures of the island with her. Eagerly, he identified many of the birds that came into view.

"Those are black guillimots. There's a tern. That handsome fellow is an osprey."

Even the smallest plant nestled in cracks on the rocky

hillside didn't escape his attention. He pointed out patches of laurel, rockwood and kelp left at high tide. He seemed in total harmony with his environment and clearly was reluctant to leave until the approaching twilight put the hillside in shadow.

Once he put his arm around her, she resisted the temptation to respond to this tenuous invitation to the impulsive kiss he had given her at the ferry dock. How could she trust herself to keep things on an even keel if she let down her guard? She didn't even look at him as she drew away and he dropped his arm from her shoulder.

When they returned to the house, she insisted on helping with the cleanup, and it was nearly nine o'clock before they got into the car to go back to the Langdons'.

"I don't suppose you'd like to take a ride with me in the morning? I need to take some photographs of an old cemetery on the island."

"A cemetery?" she echoed.

"Deputy Bill's mother's writing an article about a pioneer cemetery located on the northwestern corner of the island. She needs a couple of pictures. I've got a pretty good camera and volunteered to take them for her."

"Oh, I didn't know you were a photographer."

"I like to think so. Anyway, legend has it that some early pirates came ashore there and were buried in the cemetery along with the early settlers. You might find it interesting."

She hesitated, wanting to be with him as much as possible before she left. "I really shouldn't."

"We could go early enough so you won't miss a morning's work."

"All right."

"I meant early, like four thirty."

"Ouch," she said

When they reached the Langdon house, they were startled to see a dozen lights ablaze in the main house.

"That's Dr. Hadley's car," Brad said as he parked next to a small sedan. "The old man must be worse."

Chapter Eleven

As they walked into the house, Ashley slipped her hand in his. He could tell from the jut of her chin that she was bracing herself for spending another night in this house. As his fingers closed warmly over hers, he wondered if they could keep the distance they'd struggled all evening to maintain.

What if she invited him up to her room?

He quickly shoved the thought aside. Such speculation was pointless.

Mrs. Mertz was coming down the main staircase as they entered the front hall. Brad could tell from the housekeeper's expression she was ready to erupt like a simmering volcano.

"What is it, Mrs. Mertz?" Brad asked quickly.

"Mr. Clayton has had a relapse," she replied as her dark piercing eyes settled on Ashley. "And it's your fault!"

"Why do you say that?" Brad demanded quickly.

The woman's mouth narrowed in an ugly line. "Nurse Nigel told me everything. Miss Davis came into his room last night dressed like his late wife and this morning Mr. Clayton barely rallied enough to talk."

"I already know about the incident," Brad replied evenly.

"And if you were doing your job, Officer, she'd have already been arrested."

Brad squeezed Ashley's arm for support. "Careful, Mrs. Mertz. Don't tempt me to make an arrest for slander."

The housekeeper just lifted her nose a little higher in the air.

"Please tell Dr. Hadley we'd like to speak with him before he leaves," Brad said in his official tone. "We'll wait in the family sitting room."

He quickly guided Ashley past the scowling housekeeper.

Ashley muttered as they made their way to the southeast corner of the house, "It's that blasted nurse. She's responsible for all of this."

He was glad Ashley had filled him in about the nurse's tirade that morning, but he wasn't about to jump to any conclusion.

"She's set all this up, I know it!" Ashley insisted.

"Let's find out what the doctor has to say about Clayton before we fight any battles."

No one was in the family room. Ashley dropped down into a chair and leaned her head back against it, as if her thoughts were too heavy at the moment to hold it up.

Brad moved restlessly around the room and was relieved when Dr. Hadley joined them a few minutes later.

The doctor greeted them with a tired smile. "What was it you wanted to see me about, Officer?"

"We're concerned about Mr. Langdon and would like to hear the whole story from you."

"There's not much to tell. I was called in because Clayton suffered a blackout this morning. By the time I got here, he was conscious and talking about a vision he'd seen in the night. A kind of angel, I guess. Apparently, she floated into his room, touched him, and floated out again. Pure hallucination but terribly real to him."

Ashley opened her mouth as if to protest, but Brad intervened quickly, "I'm glad that it was only a fainting spell."

"Yes, we all are."

"What did Nurse Nigel have to say about it?"

The doctor's expression closed up, as if professional ethics prevented him from repeating anything she'd told him. Without answering, he quickly bid them good night and took his leave.

Brad could tell Ashley was seething even before she lashed out at him. "Why didn't you let me tell him that I'd experienced the same kind of so-called hallucination?"

"The time isn't right," he answered flatly.

"And when will that be?"

"When I know what in the hell is going on."

"You don't believe me."

"Yes, I do, and that's why we're going to take this slow. Don't let the suspicions of a narrow-minded housekeeper or nurse put you on the defense. You're the stranger in the house and obviously the one who's most suspect. Come on, I'll see you upstairs."

She walked stiffly beside him as they mounted the stairs to the second floor and made their way to the end of the hall.

"I'm not going to be made the scapegoat in this little charade," she declared when they reached her doorway.

"That's what it is…a charade," he assured her. "If someone's playing a game, we'll find out what the prize is. Then we'll know who the players are. In the meantime, don't do anything on your own."

He'd never felt so protective about any woman before. If there'd been any chance of convincing her to come back to his house with him, he would have given it his best shot.

"I'll pick you up before sunrise because I want to catch light rising on the old stones. Afterward, we can have breakfast and you'll still be back in time for your usual work schedule."

She nodded and looked at him in a way that invited a lot more than a good night pat on the arm. As he gathered her close, a spark of desire flamed in her eyes. Her demanding response to his kisses left them both breathless. He could have made love to her then. Her defenses were down and her inviting bed was only a few feet away.

"Whoa," he said huskily as he drew back. "I'd better say good night."

He just stood there as she searched his face. Then she went into the bedroom and shut the door.

ASHLEY LISTENED to his retreating footsteps and chided herself for welcoming his kisses and embraces like a foolish miser filling a bank with dead-end memories. Why was she so foolish to create another emptiness in her life? As she got ready for bed, her mind played over and over the time she'd spent with Brad Taylor. She ought to cut her losses now before her emotions took a permanent beating—if it wasn't already too late!

In spite of all the logical arguments to the contrary, she was ready and waiting for him the next morning when the first gray line of dawn edged the night's mantle of darkness. Dressed warmly in jeans, sweater and a lined jacket, she went down the front steps when the headlights of his car flashed through dense, encroaching woods bordering the road.

She slipped into the passenger seat even before he had the chance to get out of the car and hold the door open for her.

"Well, good morning," Brad said, a slight surprise in his greeting. He was obviously pleased she was ready and waiting.

"You didn't think I'd show, did you?"

"It's pretty early."

"Not when you've lain awake half the night."

He shot her a quick look. "Nothing else happened, did it?"

"Not that I know about. I'm glad to get away before the household begins to stir."

"When I take you back, I'll see what I can find out."

The road that crossed the island grew narrower as

they drove north. Dark green, nearly black trees engulfed the car in shadows and scattered cottages were only indistinct forms in the pale light of a gray dawn.

Ashley was thankful for the warmth of the heater and the reassuring presence of the man sitting beside her. The only thing that appealed to her about the early morning excursion was his company. As she glanced at his thoughtful expression, she wondered if he was even aware of her presence.

"Do you do this often?"

"Only when I have an excuse," he admitted sending her a quick smile. "I got my first camera when I was ten and was hooked, I guess. The island is ever-changing from morning to night, season to season. Taking pictures is a good pastime."

Once they left the dense forest, the ground leveled off quickly. The eastern horizon was growing lighter with a hint of a new day, but wispy fog still hovered above the flat, sparsely vegetated ground.

"Here we are," Brad said, nodding to the area ahead.

Ashley looked at the eerie scene, and her first reaction was to stay in the car. The old cemetery was an ugly patch of land, stark and abandoned. A few dead birch trees remained, standing upright like twisted skeletons. Irregular stones like black sentinels marked the graves. Just looking at them, Ashley felt like an unwanted intruder in a place that should not be violated. Reluctantly, she got out of the car.

Brad seemed unaware of her reaction. Obviously, he had graduated to more professional equipment since his first little camera. He carried a tripod and light meter, and the camera he slung over his shoulder was an expensive one.

Glancing at the lightening sky, he said, "I'd better hurry. I want to catch the flickering shadows and the mist on the tombstones. One of those dead trees would look good in the background."

A cold mist drifted around Ashley's legs as she followed him. Some of the slightly raised and sunken graves had granite headstones, but others were not marked. She stopped short every time she thought she might be stepping on someone's buried remains.

She tried to summon up some interest in the readable epitaphs, but most of them were simply names and dates. Many were simply marked Unknown. She needed a better knowledge of the history of the island to appreciate this bit of Greystone history.

Brad took pictures of the brooding, shadowy burial ground from a half-dozen locations. When a blush of tangerine colors was beginning to spread quickly across the sky from the rising sun, he moved his location and took some more.

"I guess that's it," he finally said with satisfaction. "I think I got some good contrasting shots."

"You seem to know what you're doing."

"We'll see. Now let's go get some breakfast."

Before they reached the car, a fast-walking little woman hurried down the road in their direction. She waved and shouted something which the nearby surf drowned out.

"That's Dora Hunskut. Bill's mother." Brad laughed. "Checking up on me, I'll bet. She's anointed herself as the unofficial guardian of the cemetery. Always on the lookout for vandalism by careless and insensitive tourists. Dora's in her seventies, but spunky as all get out. You don't want to cross her."

"I was hoping I'd get here earlier," she said, slightly out of breath as she reached them. She had a baseball cap on her frizzy gray hair and wore a faded denim jacket and jeans. "Did you get the pictures?"

"Sure did. Got some good ones, I think. Dora, I'd like you to meet Ashley Davis, she's—"

"I know who she is." She smile broadly at Ashley as she held out her tanned, veined hand. "Landsakes, the whole island knows by now. What a nice surprise. I didn't know Brad would have company this early in the morning, but it's no matter. I've got enough breakfast fixing waiting."

"Dora, we—" Brad began.

"Now you hush up." She shook a finger at him. "I've been waiting for a chance to meet up with this young lady. There are plenty of things she should know about you." She winked at Ashley. "I've got a parcel of stories about the island's esteemed police officer."

"I'd love to hear them."

They laughed. Brad groaned.

The distance to the Hunskuts' was less than a mile from the cemetery. The simple Cape Cod style home was warm and inviting. A sign, ROOMS FOR RENT, hung from a decorative piece of driftwood at the front gate.

"Do you have any renters, Dora?" Brad asked as they entered the house through the front door. He knew Bill's salary wasn't enough to provide many extra comforts.

"Not now. But it's been a busy summer. Bill and I have had our hands full."

Brad knew his deputy and his widowed mother worked hard to offer the best bed-and-breakfast on the island. Even though most tourists didn't want to stay more than one or two days, sometimes Dora was able to rent out a room for the whole summer or winter season.

"Bill has left already," Dora told him. "He said he'd open up the office and then get a bite of breakfast at the café. Either he's tired of his ma's cooking, or he's sweet on that new waitress." She put a thoughtful finger up to her cheek. "I wonder which it is?"

They laughed as they followed her to the kitchen. While Dora bustled around fixing enough food for a houseful of guests, Ashley and Brad sat down at the round kitchen table.

"You have a very cheery home," Ashley told her. "I wish I were staying here instead of with the Langdons."

"Well, move. I've got a nice front room, newly decorated."

"I would if I wasn't just about finished. Only a few more days."

"Maybe you'll be staying longer than you think. Right, Brad?" She shot him a knowing look.

He silently groaned. All they needed was an over-eager matchmaker to ruin the tenuous relationship between them. He quickly changed the subject.

"Dora, tell Ashley about the painter who stayed here while he spent several months on the island."

"An Englishman, Latimore Baines. He was here for a whole spring and summer almost twenty-five years ago."

She hurried into the next room as he knew she would and brought back two landscape paintings. Dora could never resist the opportunity to brag she owned two original oil paintings.

"I took these instead of rent. This one shows the view of the beach and ocean from our veranda. And this one Latimore painted down at the wharf." She beamed. "I guess both of them are worth some money now that the man's dead."

"The name is vaguely familiar," Ashley told her. "But I'm not very knowledgeable about modern landscape painters."

"Oh, Latimore did other things. While he was here he painted a portrait of Samantha Langdon."

"Oh, I've seen that portrait," Ashley said in surprise. "It's hanging in Jonathan Langdon's office."

"It's a beauty, isn't it? Latimore was real proud of his work. He used my sewing room for the sittings. The place smelled of paint and turpentine for months afterward."

"Jonathan said his wife had it done for his birthday, but was killed before she could give it to him."

Brad watched Dora's mouth close tightly as if she were holding something back. "You must have gotten to know Samantha pretty well while Latimore was doing her portrait," Brad said casually.

Dora gave her glasses a shove back on her nose.

"Maybe better than I wanted to. She was always chatting about some social affair or another. She should have been home taking care of her little baby instead of posing like some queen for her portrait."

Brad knew there was more and if Dora was in a chatty mood, he would encourage her. "No one seems to know what Samantha was doing on the mainland the night she was killed in that automobile accident. I guess there was a hint of suspicion she wasn't alone."

"I'm not one to speak ill of the dead," Dora said, trying to defend herself before she did exactly that. "The truth is, the portrait was not intended for her husband. Latimore told me in confidence she was having it painted for someone else."

"Really? Do you know who?"

"Latimore never said. He hadn't quite finished the portrait when she was killed. He hadn't been paid for it and when Latimore showed it to Jonathan Langdon, he thought his wife had commissioned it for him and he readily paid the agreed-upon amount."

"And you don't have any idea who that lucky man might have been?" Brad prodded.

"Why would I know? We didn't exactly run in the same circles." She shrugged. "You'd have to find someone a lot closer to what went on at the Langdon compound than me to get at the truth."

Someone like Mary Sandrow? Was any of this related to the possible blackmail payments being made monthly to Samantha's old nurse?

"It's hard to believe the happenings in such a

prominent family could rival a TV soap opera," Ashley said, shaking her head.

"I've thought about writing a book about the Langdons," Dora confessed. "It would be a lot more exciting and profitable than writing articles for historical magazines. The police even interviewed me when Pamela died of the overdose."

"Really? Why?" Brad had never looked into the official accounts of Pamela Langdon's death because the investigation had been closed nearly two years before he moved back to the island.

Dora leaned forward in her kitchen chair. "Timothy Templeton took a room with me for a week after the suicide. The authorities wouldn't let him leave the island and the Langdons wouldn't let him set foot on their property. If Timothy hadn't been on the yacht that night, he'd have been a cooked goose, for sure. I think Jonathan Langdon would have strung him up to the nearest tree himself. As soon as the authorities released him, Timothy packed his cheap suitcase and left."

"Where'd he go?" Brad asked.

"I don't know. Do you think I'd have to get Timothy's permission? Just the Langdon name would sell a lot of books," she said excitedly. "If I only put in the facts, who could object?"

"Jonathan Langdon, for one," Brad warned her. "He's not likely to agree to any tell-all about the family, especially about his wife's and daughter's untimely deaths."

Dora set her jaw and he knew that anything he said

would only stiffen her determination. Unfortunately, his own suspicions were too nebulous to use as an argument against her proposed literary project. He purposefully changed the subject.

"I think I got some good shots of the cemetery. I'll get them to you as soon as they're developed."

They left a few minutes later.

"Nice lady," Ashley commented as they headed back to the Langdon compound. "But she didn't keep her promise. I was looking forward to hearing some tall tales about you and Bill."

Brad chuckled. "We gave Dora some gray hairs, all right. But I'll tell you what. I'll tell you a few myself if you'll have dinner at my place tonight."

"You're cooking?"

"Do I detect skepticism in your tone?"

"What's on the menu?" A smile flickered on the edge of her lips.

"That's a surprise. I'll pick you up about seven."

After seeing her inside the house, he headed back to the office and found Bill working on a monthly report for the mainland office.

"You and Ashley Davis were up pretty early this morning, mom told me," Bill said. "Ms. Davis doesn't look the type to get out of bed before noon unless—"

"Can it, Bill," Brad said gruffly. "We've got work to do."

"What's up?"

"Do you know if Timothy Templeton has been back to the island any time in the two years since Pamela Langdon's death?"

He frowned. "Not that I know about. Knowing Greystone's gossip line, I'm sure someone would have spread the word if he showed up."

"He could have visited the Langdon compound without being noticed. Anyone who docks a boat at the pier below the mansion has access to the property."

"What are you thinking, boss?"

"If Timothy learned that Pamela's things were being inventoried and put up for sale, it's possible he might be worried about something coming to light that would incriminate him. He could have panicked and assaulted Lorrie to make sure she didn't continue the assignment."

"Wow, that's really a stretch, isn't it, boss?"

"Let's run some checks and see if we can find out what he's been doing and where he's been keeping himself."

"As I recall, he didn't have much of a family," Bill offered. "I remember there was some question about where Timothy was getting money to hang out with the idle rich like Pamela Langdon."

Brad sat down at his computer. He used every official resource available in an effort to collect recent data on Timothy Templeton and came up empty.

"He couldn't have just disappeared," Bill argued.

"Maybe he was afraid the Langdons would hunt him down in retaliation for Pamela's death. For the last two years, he could have been living with a false identity."

"Why would he gamble on coming back for any reason? That doesn't make sense, boss."

"Yes, it does," Brad argued. "We just don't have all the pieces."

Chapter Twelve

When Ashley came down the stairs a little after seven o'clock, she heard Brad's voice. She knew she was late. Somehow, the whole day had gotten away from her. Happily, she'd made headway in packing up the remaining garments and only a few details remained before the entire collection would be ready for shipping.

She hadn't stopped to shower and change clothes until after six-thirty and then there was the problem of what to wear. For some reason, she wanted to look special and a dozen casual outfits hanging in her closet at home would have been perfect. It was ironic that she finally found someone on a foggy island who made her want to wear them. Unfortunately, at the moment her wardrobe was so limited she had to settle for a pale blue knit dress she'd hurriedly packed because it didn't wrinkle. The cardigan sweater she'd bought in Portland would have to do for a wrap. She added pearl earrings and a narrow matching choker and gave herself a quick nod of approval as her trim figure reflected back at her from the gold-framed mirror.

As she hurried down the stairs, she chided herself for a bubbling of adolescent excitement. She'd been wined and dined in some of the finest restaurants on both coasts, but strangely enough, a casual meal with Brad Taylor suddenly outdistanced them all.

Brad was in the main living room with Paul and Jonathan. The three men stood in front of an open bar with drinks in their hands. Brad looked perfectly at ease and incredibly handsome wearing dark slacks and an open-neck blue sweater that showed off the muscles in his arms and shoulders.

At her entrance, he gave her a welcoming smile. "Ready?"

"Sorry to keep you waiting."

"No problem," he assured her.

"You're looking lovely tonight, Ashley," the lawyer said in his man-about-town manner. "Won't you join us for a quick drink before you hit the island's bright lights?"

Jonathan nodded in agreement. "What would you like, Ashley?"

"Thank you but I'll pass."

"Well then, I guess we'll be off," Brad responded. "Jonathan, if your brother, Philip, shows up, will you tell him I'd like to see him. I think he would know if someone else is using the boat dock."

Paul Fontaine frowned as he said, "I really don't know where you're going with this."

"Neither do I," Brad admitted. "But that's the way things go in police work sometimes. You keep pulling on a string until you find out what's tied to it."

Both men were scowling as they left the room and Brad told her quietly, "I think both Jonathan and Paul wanted to forbid you to go out tonight."

"Why would they care?"

"Maybe personal reasons as far as Paul is concerned. He obviously considers himself a ladies' man. With Jonathan it might be a fear that the two of us may tumble onto something that would threaten the Langdons' good name."

"It's a little late for them to be worried about that, isn't it?" Her tone was testy. She didn't want to spend the evening talking about the Langdons.

He shot her a quick look. "Sorry. I guess I'm not very good at this dating thing."

"It depends upon whether this evening is business or pleasure."

"Definitely pleasure."

On the drive to his house, he confessed he'd been anxious she might decide not to come. "I'm finding it hard to believe that you're really leaving—for good."

She didn't answer. Tonight might be all they would ever have and she wasn't going to fill it with regret. There'd be time enough for that later.

The dog gave them an enthusiastic welcome and was obviously interested in the sacks containing carryout dinners Brad had picked up at the café.

"Down boy! I'll feed you first and get you out of the way. I'll be back in a minute," he told Ashley as he left her in the front room and disappeared into the kitchen.

The room was still as ugly and stark as before, and

Ashley felt a stab of disappointment that Brad didn't seem to notice how drab it was. If she had to spend much time in such bleak surroundings, she'd dry up and blow away. What did they have in common except the unfortunate circumstances that had brought them together?

"There's kind of a picnic area at the back of the house," he told her as he came back into the room. "It doesn't have a view of the water but it's pleasant. I thought we'd eat there."

Apparently he'd accepted the fact that she wasn't all that crazy about being close to the pounding ocean and its rugged shoreline. After shutting Rusty up in the bedroom, he led the way out the back door and around the corner of the house, where he'd spread a blanket out on the ground. Their dinner was set out on paper plates.

"I'm not much on entertaining—"

"It's fine," she assured him quickly as she eased down on the ground. She'd made a big mistake in deciding what to wear. She could feel the dampness of the ground as her clinging skirt crept up to a provocative shortness.

He poured the wine, sat down on the blanket, Indian-style, and smiled at her in a boyish way that fired her imagination. What if they'd met when they were younger? What if he'd been her very first date? Her very first love? Would she have been pliable enough to fit into the pattern of his life before she'd committed to her own?

"You have a choice of the Rockcove Café special, baked lobster and creamed pasta, or their next favorite, breaded veal and hash brown potatoes."

"I'll take the lobster."

"Good choice. You won't find any that fresh anywhere…not even your famous Fisherman's Wharf. Would you really miss it all that much?"

"I like to visit different places," she hedged. "But as the saying goes, I wouldn't want to live there—"

"Or here?"

Her hand trembled slightly as she set down her glass. "I guess I'd miss the city. I don't think I'd like being cut off from the mainland any length of time."

"Well, then I guess it's a good thing you're just about ready to leave. The winters here are not what you would call friendly."

Her high spirits had taken a nosedive. Why? Why had she had such high expectations for the evening? Did she want a commitment from him, saying that his feelings had grown as deep as her own? Something inside of her rebelled at the thought she'd never know what might have been between them.

As they ate, he seemed determined to keep the conversation away from any expression of his own feelings. "Someday I want to do a little sailing. How about you?"

"If it's a cruise ship, I'm all for it."

"That's not sailing."

They tried a few more topics but didn't find one that lasted for more than a few brief exchanges. Every silence seemed weighted with unexpressed emotion. Even though they sat inches from each other on the blanket, there seemed to be an insurmountable barrier between them.

When both of them had stopped eating, even though there was more food left on their plates, he asked, "Would you like coffee and dessert?"

"No, thanks. I'm quite satisfied."

They carried their empty dishes back to the small kitchen. Despite Brad's protests, Ashley insisted upon washing the wineglasses and silverware. The tiny work space was crowded with the both of them.

"Whoa," he said when they collided. His hands went quickly around her waist to steady her. The sudden physical intimacy took them both by surprise. Their eyes locked, and his breath quickened as suddenly as her own.

She looked into his eyes, so often guarded but now soft with longing. She touched his full mouth with a fingertip and laid her hand upon his cheek. The decision was made without her realizing it. Tonight she would accept his love as if it belonged to her. Tonight she would not think about tomorrow, nor the emptiness ahead. As he lowered his lips to capture hers, her whole body quivered with unbelievable hunger.

They had been building up to this moment from their first stormy meeting. His small bedroom held the faint light of twilight as they lay together.

"I love you," he whispered, kissing her eyelids and letting his hands caress the rosy crests of her breasts.

As they came together, giving and taking, a shared fulfillment went beyond desire…beyond caresses… beyond promises…beyond understanding.

She drifted off to sleep, warm and content in the

circle of his arms. Even in the throes of contentment, she came awake with a jolt.

"What is it?" he asked.

She sat up. "I…don't know."

"You're here, with me. Remember?" He quickly turned on a bedside lamp.

She gave him a slightly embarrassed smile and then leaned forward and lightly kissed him. "I remember."

His hand slipped down to rest on the fullness of a breast. "So do I."

She pulled away and said, "It's nearly midnight. I'd love to stay but—"

"Are you afraid of gossip?" he chided.

"Not for myself."

He frowned. "Then what? I don't care what anyone says."

"Not now, but things change," she said as she began getting dressed.

"Okay, but I've got something to show you before I take you back."

After they were dressed, he turned on a light in a small room across the hall. As Ashley followed him through the doorway, she felt as if she had suddenly been transformed into another dimension.

She couldn't believe her eyes. Every space on the four walls was covered with photographs of the island: birds, rocks, waves, trees, clouds, water, boats, fishermen, and dirty-faced children playing in the sand. She was speechless.

"What do you think?"

"You took all of these?"

"And a few hundred more," he admitted rather sheepishly. "I guess you could call it an addiction. Dora Hunskut got me started. She always needed photos to go with those freelance articles of hers. Mostly travel and historical magazines," he said as he indicated a small stack on a scarred-up desk. "She always gives me a copy."

"I think that's wonderful. Do you get credit for the photographs?"

"Sometimes, but that's not what's important to me." He handed her a large manila envelope. "Here's my reward."

She drew out the photos he'd taken that morning at the cemetery and her breath caught. She couldn't believe the power contained in every picture.

Early morning shadows seemed to come alive like dark spirits hovering over the ugly graves and tombstones. Twisted, barren branches of dead trees made a black tracery against a gray misty sky. The slowly emerging sunlight in some of the prints was like a creeping light fighting the dark forces of the cemetery.

She could see that in the progression of photos he'd taken a theme began to emerge. It was as if the power of death in the shadowy pictures was somehow defeated in the full brightness of a sunrise. Each photograph was powerful by itself and, together, they were a modern tapestry of light overcoming death.

"What do you think?" he prodded.

She was at a loss what to say. The magnificent talent he seemed to dismiss so casually had left her speechless.

She couldn't find the words to express the deep, emotional message he'd captured through the lens of his camera.

"What's wrong?" He frowned, obviously disappointed in her silent reaction. "I told you this is just a pastime of mine. I'm not out to win any blue ribbons."

"You're very good," she said in a reverent tone. "Professional enough to submit your work to any exhibition."

"No, thanks." He tossed the envelope down on his desk.

"Why not?"

"I like taking photos. I like hanging them on my walls, but making a business out of them doesn't appeal to me."

"Why not?" she repeated. His reasoning completely escaped her.

"I'm not sure. If my photographs help Dora sell an article or two, that's good enough and I'm happy."

"Are you really?"

The question seemed to stop him for a moment. Then he pulled her close, "Well, living alone isn't all that great. Do you think we could do something about that?"

As his hands gently caressed her, she tried to ignore the spurt of sexual energy that shot through her. Was this his way of asking her to stay on the island with him? Marry him? How could she tell him that she'd curl up and die if she spent more than a few weeks at a time on this island he loved so much.

"What's wrong? I don't understand," he said as she pulled away. "If you and I—"

"It wouldn't last."

"Why not?"

"The term *incompatible* comes to mind."

"I thought we'd found something worth keeping."

She moistened her lips and quoted, "One night of love does not a future make."

They stood looking at each other across a chasm suddenly too deep to cross. "I didn't realize you were so committed to your present way of life," he said.

"And you to yours," she countered just as firmly. She turned away and went back into the bedroom to gather her things.

When they left Brad's house a few minutes later, the weather was in harmony with their turbulent feelings. A fierce wind assaulted the island as storm clouds swept inland. Ashley's thoughts and feelings were too heavy for polite conversation, and the enveloping dense fog kept Brad's attention on driving.

When they arrived at the Langdon compound, he held her firmly against the buffeting winds as they made their way from the car to the house and quickly ushered her inside.

"Brad, I—"

"Don't."

Without another word, he turned and left her standing there. A moment later, the lights on his police cruiser flickered briefly across a window and then disappeared.

As Ashley mounted the stairs, rising winds were like wild beasts beating on the outside of the mansion. Swatches of white mist writhed against windows like ghostly hands pleading to get in. Her chest tightened as she cast furtive looks behind her and quickened her steps.

The dark corridor leading to her room seemed more ominous than ever at two o'clock in the morning but as she neared her bedroom, a ribbon of light showed under her closed door.

"I must have remembered to leave a light on," she murmured.

As she opened the door and stepped inside, a blast of cold air assaulted her. The raging storm seemed to be sweeping through the room. Then she saw why.

The door to the widow's walk was open! Hurriedly she slammed it shut and locked it.

As she turned away from the door, a woman with long blond hair lying on her bed sat up and stared unseeing at Ashley. Slowly she stood, arranged the eggshell peignoir that flowed around her silver slippered feet and brushed back a false hairpiece caught in a butterfly scarf.

Ashley gave a choked gasp. It was Ellen Brenden!

Chapter Thirteen

Was she sleepingwalking? Hypnotized?

Ashley watched in mesmerized silence as Ellen's unseeing eyes passed over her. Slowly she turned, then ran across the bedroom and out into the hall.

Ashley bounded out the door after her. "Ellen! Ellen! Wait."

Ellen didn't slow down, nor give any sign that she'd heard, but continued racing down the hall with her white robe and long hair flowing out behind her.

Ashley knew she should alert someone to Ellen's strangc behavior as soon as possible. Who? How? Would anyone in the household believe her without more evidence than her say-so? The finger of doubt had already been pointed at her as the one who was roving about the house at night, causing the old man to have a relapse.

Determined to clear herself, she raced after Ellen. Because Ashley had become slightly familiar with some of the bisecting corridors and stairways, she was easily able keep up with Ellen for a short time. Too soon, all familiarity ended. The chase led down to a lower floor where Ashley had never been before.

SHE HAD NO IDEA where they were in the house when Ellen suddenly slowed to a walk. She approached an open door where an overhead chandelier sent a radius of bright light around a spacious bedroom.

Ashley remained in the doorway and watched Ellen move in mechanical fashion around the room. In unemotional, trance-like movements, she discarded the white robe, blond wig and silver slippers. After she had carefully placed them on a shelf in the closet, she firmly closed the door. Clad in a plain cotton grannie nightgown she'd been wearing underneath the outer garment, she lay down in the bed and closed her eyes.

Ashley remained in the doorway until Ellen's breathing took on the slow rhythms of sleep. An expression of relaxed contentment was on her face, and Ashley doubted if the woman even remembered her nightly sojourns the next morning. Ashley couldn't help but wonder what hidden torment drove Ellen to perform these sleepwalking masquerades.

Ashley quietly turned away and started on her return trek through the house. High-pitched wailing of the wind echoed down the dimly lit corridors. The strength of the storm had increased to such a level that inner walls vibrated from the assault. She hurried up several steps connecting older sections of the mansion and tried to orient herself. Tiny hall lights were dim and far between. When she came to a stairway that seemed familiar, she was confident the corridor leading to her hall was at the top—only it wasn't.

The stairs didn't lead to another corridor but ended in a small, dimly lit sitting area. She stopped short as she smelled cigarette smoke. In almost the same instant a hand reached out from the depths of a high-back chair and turned on a small lamp beside it. She couldn't see who sat there because the chair was turned away from her.

"Hello," she said in a tone that indicated a lot more poise than she felt. Her pulse quickened as a man stood up and turned around.

He took another puff on his cigarette before he spoke. "I'm sorry if I startled you. I'm Philip Langdon."

Jonathan's younger brother.

"Ashley Davis," she responded politely. She remembered Brad had said Philip Langdon had been married two or three times. Distinguishing gray sideburns harmonized with his strong masculine features, and he was quite attractive.

"Good evening, or should I say good morning?" he said with a teasing smile.

"Both, I guess."

"I've heard about you and understand you are taking over for your sister. We've all been terribly concerned about what happened to Lorrie. Unbelievable. I had the pleasure of meeting her a few days before the unfortunate incident. How is she doing?"

"Wonderfully."

"I'm glad to hear it. I'm not up-to-date on the news because I arrived after the household had already settled in for the night."

His inquiring gaze invited her to explain her own dressed-up appearance, but she wasn't about to give him the satisfaction of an explanation.

She hadn't decided how much she should say about Ellen's sleepwalking. In some ways she felt protective of Ellen Brenden, as if the Langdon men had misused her unfailing devotion. The woman had been a mother to Pamela and a nurse to Clayton; Ashley suspected she might even have been rejected by Jonathan as his second wife. In any case, she didn't know Philip Langdon well enough to trust him with Ellen's secret. She wanted to talk to Dr. Hadley first and let him decide what to do.

"The storm makes it pretty hard to sleep," she offered as a safe subject.

"You're in Pamela's old room, aren't you? That side of the house takes the brunt of any ocean storm. Strangely enough, Pamela never complained. I think she was a romantic at heart, but so was her mother." Before Ashley could respond, he abruptly changed the subject. "Let's find ourselves a nightcap. We'll wait out the storm together."

"I'm afraid I can't," she declined quickly. "I've got to get a few hours' sleep. I only need one more day to finish up everything."

"Oh, that's too bad. I thought I heard some gossip that you might be staying here for a while."

"No," she said firmly. "I'm heading back to California as soon as everything is ready for transport."

"Well, I hope you'll give me your address. We could have that nightcap in the City by the Bay."

She was about to bid him a polite good night when she realized she didn't have the foggiest idea how to get back to her side of the house. As a peal of thunder and pounding rain heralded a new assault, she swallowed her pride.

"Would you mind showing me the way? I took a couple of wrong turns tonight, and frankly I don't know how I turned up here."

"My pleasure," he said, and the way he slipped his arm through hers, she wondered if she'd invited more than she could handle.

No doubt rich and handsome, Philip Langdon was comfortable in his role as protector of the fairer sex. Unlike his brother, he exuded a simmering sexuality. As a young man, he must have been devastatingly attractive to more than one susceptible female. Everything Dora Hunskut had said about Samantha suggested that there had been another man in her life. Was that man Philip Langdon? *Could Samantha's portrait have been intended for her husband's brother?*

Ashley suddenly felt ill at ease in his company. As soon as they reached a familiar second-floor corridor, she stopped and eased away from his guiding arm.

"My room is just ahead. Thanks for the company. I'll not keep you from your nightcap any longer."

"I'll gladly see you to your door."

"No need." She gave him a smile and a dismissive wave of her hand. "See you in the morning."

As she walked away, she forced herself not to look back and see if he was following her down the hall to her room.

BRAD DROVE BACK to his house after leaving Ashley. He let Rusty out for a short run in the foul weather and then got back in the car and headed for his office. He knew storms like the one building always took their toll on the island. In such high winds, boats broke away from their moorings, trees were uprooted, loose rocks created mud slides and weakened structures collapsed. Dr. Hadley would be kept busy handling minor medical needs and arranging for transportation to the mainland for the serious injuries. Brad knew that if the demands for help were more than he and Bill could supply, he'd have to call in additional help from the mainland. Everything depended upon how fast the storm would move northward.

The office was dark and cold when Brad let himself inside. He changed into a spare uniform, put on a fleece-lined jacket, and threw himself down on the bunk bed provided for overnight visitors. He needed a few hours' sleep, but as he lay there, wide awake and thinking about Ashley, the bittersweet hours he'd spent with her created warring emotions he wasn't ready to handle. He'd been a fool, he knew that. He'd made assumptions based on his own feelings and desires. He had ignored the very traits in Ashley that had caused him to fall in love with her. She was her own woman, with a purpose and dedication. He should have been smart enough to recognize and accept her independence from the first moment he'd met her. Instead, he had assumed she would gladly remain on the island and play house with him. Damn, he'd misjudged the situation all around.

Too keyed up to even catch a couple of hours of sleep, he got up, went to his computer and contacted the mainland for a weather report. It wasn't good.

The day turned out to be the nightmare he had expected. By the time the café across the street opened, he'd already received several calls for assistance and had alerted Bill and two emergency volunteer deputies to help cover them. He was grateful that about midafternoon, a valiant sun sent feeble rays of light through dissipating clouds and the storm moved on.

Brad had just returned to the office from one of the calls when Dora Hunskut telephoned.

"Bill is still out," he told her when he recognized her voice. "I think he's helping Old Man Benson collect his half-drowned chickens. The whole hen house floated away like Noah's ark."

"It's not Bill, I want," she said in a strained voice.

"You sound tense, Dora. What's the matter? Are you all right?" he asked quickly.

He could hear her taking a couple of deep breaths. "It's just that I've had kind of a shock."

"What happened, Dora?"

"It's the cemetery."

"What about it?"

"I walked up there to see if the saplings I planted this spring survived the storm."

Brad knew how Dora babied those trees. She'd be upset if she lost them, but there were worse things happening all over the island.

"I'm sorry if you lost them."

"Oh, no they made it through fine." She hesitated. "It's that large dead tree, the one a few hundred feet from the road. You know the one?"

"Yes," Brad answered, puzzled.

"It fell over."

"I'm not surprised," Brad said, feeling a wave of relief. "It's been dead for as long as I can remember. Don't worry about it, Dora. We'll have someone cut it up and remove the dead wood."

"It's not that!"

"Then what, Dora?"

"When the tree fell over," she said in a shaky voice, "the roots pulled out of the ground and…"

"And..?" Brad prodded in an encouraging tone.

"There was a body there."

"Maybe someone was buried under the tree years ago when it was alive," Brad reasoned in a calm voice.

"The clothes and remains looked too new. And I…and I…saw something else beside the skeleton."

"What, Dora?"

"A cheap cardboard suitcase," she said in a cracked voice. "The kind…the kind that Timothy Templeton was carrying the day he left my house."

Brad had a hard time finding his own voice. "I'll check it out, Dora."

"It can't be him, can it?"

"I'll check it out, Dora," he repeated as a rush of heat surged through him.

As Brad drove to the cemetery, he put unanswered questions about Timothy in a different perspective. Maybe Timothy Templeton had never left the island. What if an autopsy proved he had met a violent death before Pamela's funeral? He was convinced that this unexpected discovery ended his fruitless search for the whereabouts of the young man.

A cold prickling between Brad's shoulder blades accompanied his next thought.

Was a murderer waiting, ready and willing to strike again?

When he got to the cemetery, the shallow grave was just as Dora had described. The roots of the fallen tree had exposed a skeleton in decaying men's clothing. The cheap suitcase Dora had described had disintegrated.

Brad didn't touch anything. A forensic team from the state medical examiner's office would have to be notified.

"You look like hell," his deputy said frankly when Brad returned to the office. "How much sleep did you get last night?"

"Not enough," Brad answered shortly and told him about Bill's mother's discovery. "I'd bet a month's salary that it's Timothy Templeton."

Bill gave a low whistle. "How long has he been dead?"

"We'll have to ask the forensic team to determine

when and how he died but I wouldn't be surprised if the young man wasn't in his grave before they had the funeral to bury Pamela."

"Holy cow! What do we do now?"

"I'm going to pay the Langdons a visit. I want to see their reaction to the discovery before they hear about the grave from someone else."

He took the patrol car and made a quick stop at his house to shower and change clothes. The remains of last night's dinner and the lingering scent of Ashley's perfume in the bedroom did nothing to improve his mood. The prospect of seeing her again, even in the frame of official business, disturbed him at levels he wouldn't have thought possible. What more could they say to each other?

He was still wondering the same thing when he arrived at the Langdons' and Clara answered the door. When she saw who it was, she said, "Everyone's about to sit down for dinner. I'll tell them you're here."

Almost immediately, Ellen Brenden appeared and greeted him with a slight questioning lift of an eyebrow. "Good evening, Officer."

"I'm sorry for the interruption," he quickly apologized. "It escaped me completely that it might be your dinner hour."

"We're eating early tonight."

"If you don't mind, I'll just wait instead of coming back."

"Have you dined already?" she asked. "Maybe you

would like to join us?" She lowered her voice. "The usual table conversation is boring, boring."

I can fix that, Brad thought and quickly accepted her invitation. What could be better timing than dropping the bombshell in the middle of the dining room table and watching what happened?

Ellen ushered him into the dining room and said brightly, "We have a guest."

A stunned silence from everyone seated at the table greeted the announcement. Jonathan's frown was a mixture of irritation and speculation. Philip Langdon and Paul Fontaine sitting across from Ashley, exchanged glances. Ashley visibly paled when she saw him.

Ellen indicated Brad should take a chair next to Ashley and motioned to Clara to set another place. Mrs. Mertz scowled and left the dining room. Brad was surprised to see Philip Langdon.

Ellen smiled a little smugly as she sat down in her chair at the foot of the table. "Isn't it nice Officer Taylor could join us?"

The weighted silence was almost unbearable.

"I appreciate the invitation," Brad responded politely.

He couldn't imagine what Ashley was thinking. She was sitting close enough for him to be aware of her every breath. The familiar scent of her perfume taunted him. Surely, she didn't think he'd barged in like this to embarrass her. She had given him the impression that she didn't eat with the family all that regularly. He was sorry that tonight was one of the exceptions, but it was too late to do anything about it now.

Sitting at the head of the table, Jonathan seemed determined to ignore the police officer's intrusion. He gave his attention to the bisque soup, and leg of lamb entrée.

Philip waited until the meal was under way before addressing Brad directly. "Is there some reason you're honoring us with your presence tonight?"

Paul Fontaine quickly spoke up quickly. "You're wearing your uniform, so this visit must be official."

"In a way, it is."

"You have some news…about Lorrie's attacker?" Ellen asked, leaning forward excitedly.

"No," Brad answered quickly. He didn't want to get Ashley's hopes up. He'd hoped to wait to launch his bombshell until he could better gauge its impact. It wasn't to be.

Jonathan's fist slammed down on the table and everybody jumped. "Enough! State your business, sir!"

Brad slowly laid down his fork. "What I have to tell all of you is pretty shocking! Maybe I should wait until after dinner—" He let his gaze travel around the table to gauge their reactions.

"Our appetites are already spoiled." Philip's tone was as cutting as a steak knife.

Brad hesitated. "Maybe we should excuse the ladies?"

"No," Ashley and Ellen replied in unison.

"All right. We made a gruesome discovery this morning." He paused. Sometimes just a flicker of an eyelid could betray guilt, but all three men just seemed to be waiting for him to continue.

"The storm uprooted a dead tree in the cemetery and exposed a body buried there."

"Oh, no," Ashley gasped as if she were remembering their early morning visit.

"It wasn't one of the pioneer graves," he said.

Jonathan gave a dismissing wave of his hand. "I fail to see why you're bringing this ghoulish discovery to our attention."

"What made you think we would be the least bit interested in this kind of macabre happening?" Philip demanded in a disgusted tone.

"How gruesome," Ellen said with a shiver.

Only Fontaine kept his eyes steadily focused on Brad's face.

"There's more, isn't there, Officer?"

"I'm afraid so. The grave appears to be only a few years old. A cheap suitcase buried with the corpse may reveal his identity. Apparently it is similar to the one Timothy Templeton was carrying the last time he was seen."

A frigid stillness enveloped the dining room for a moment, then Ellen jumped to her feet and bound out of the room.

Ashley shoved back her chair and followed her. When Ashley caught up with her in the hall, she quickly put an arm around Ellen's trembling shoulders.

"It's all right...it's all right," she murmured as Ellen continued walking, hunched over and sobbing until they reached the family living room.

When Ellen dropped down on a sofa and covered her

face, Ashley quickly sat down beside her, trying to remember if she'd heard about any special connection between Pamela's fiancé and her aunt.

"I'm sorry, Ellen," she said gently. "This must be a terrible shock."

"Not really," she said in a choked voice. "I've been afraid of something like this for a long time."

"You have?" Ashley wasn't even sure she wanted to know why. She'd experienced enough emotional trauma on Greystone Island to last her a lifetime.

"It's my nephew, Kent," Ellen sobbed.

Ashley stiffened. Something ominous in Ellen's tone made her wary of becoming a confidante.

Brad should be listening to all of this, not me.

Ellen took a deep breath as if what she was going to say demanded every bit of effort. "When Timothy got engaged to Pamela, a lot of drinking and gambling went on during those yachting parties. Kent usually had to drop out of the poker games when the stakes got too high, but one night he won big and collected an enormous IOU from Timothy. Kent was deliriously happy and promised to give me back every dollar I'd loaned him when he collected from Timothy." Her voice broke. "He's really a good boy. I've done my best to help him all I can. Kent is family, and I think he really loves me."

"I'm sure he does," Ashley said in a reassuring tone even though she sincerely doubted the basis for his affection. As much as Ellen had given to everyone else, she seemed to have received very little expression of love in return.

Ellen straightened up and after taking a deep breath she looked Ashley in the eye. "The night Pamela died, Kent and Timothy had a big blowup. Timothy refused to pay the gambling debt and accused Kent of cheating. He even convinced the other poker players to turn on Kent. They told him he wasn't welcome in their company anymore. You can see how devastated he was, can't you?"

Ashley nodded.

"Kent swore to get even." Her voice trailed off into a whisper. "I guess he did."

Chapter Fourteen

Brad learned very little about Timothy's relationship with the three men as they gathered in the living room after the explosive dinner. As far as he could tell, none of them would be mourning the young man's demise. All of them seemed open about their dislike of Pamela's fiancé.

Jonathan was the most vitriolic in his remarks. "The world is better off without him. I only wish whoever had planted him in that grave had done it sooner." He swallowed hard. "Maybe my Pamela would be alive today."

"You should have done something yourself, Jonathan," his brother lashed out. "God knows, there was enough warning. You knew about the drug parties. How did you expect her to keep clean? The poor innocent little fool thought she was in love with the bastard."

"It's easy to have hindsight," Fontaine offered as a way of lowering the tension between the two brothers. "Both of you had her best interests at heart. She was strong-willed like her mother. We all knew that."

"What are you going to do about this, Taylor?"

Philip demanded in a tone that indicated he didn't put much hope in anything constructive being done by the island's policeman.

"Find out who's responsible," Brad answered evenly.

Fontaine nodded in agreement. "I wouldn't be surprised if you don't find enough suspects coming out of the woodwork from Templeton's past to keep you busy for quite a while."

"Oh, it may not take as long you might think," Brad offered pointedly. "Sometimes you don't have to go too far afield to find the answer you're looking for."

There was a dead silence. Before any of the men could respond to his insinuation that the solution to Timothy's death might be close by, Ashley appeared in the doorway.

Instead of coming into the room, she waited for Brad to join her. He quickly excused himself.

"We need to talk," she said and he could tell from her solemn expression it wasn't going to be a cozy little chat.

"Let's find some privacy."

The weather was too inclement to go outside. The way things were between them, Brad knew going up to her room wasn't an option. When he saw the door to the library open across the hall, he said, "Let's talk in there."

As he put a guiding hand on her arm, he could feel tight muscular tension in her body. Was she steaming because of the way he'd handled his announcement at dinner, or was she just furious with him, period?

After he flipped on an overhead light, they crossed the room to a grouping of furniture in front of the dark fireplace. If anyone had been sitting there recently enjoying any of the books lining the shelves from floor to ceiling, there was no evidence of it. The room had a dank, musty smell that matched its chilly temperature.

"Okay," he said as he eased down on a leather couch beside her. "Let's have it."

He was prepared for a lashing tirade about the insensitive way he'd delivered the shocking news. What she had to say took him totally by surprise.

"Ellen is convinced that her nephew, Kent, killed Timothy Templeton."

"She is? Why?"

He listened carefully as Ashley told him what Ellen had said about the gambling debt that Timothy had refused to pay. "Kent vowed to get even."

Brad digested this startling revelation for a long minute before he replied evenly, "That doesn't mean he killed the guy." He wasn't about to jump to any conclusions…not on the assumptions of an emotional aunt.

"But he could have," Ashley insisted.

"I'll have to do some investigating. Check on Kent's whereabouts the last time Timothy was seen alive. It'll take a little time. I hope Ellen isn't going to go to pieces on us."

"I think she already has." Ashley's voice faltered. "I discovered she's our ghostly phantom."

"When? How?" He stared at her. "Are you sure?"

"Positive."

He reached over, took her hand in his as she told him how she'd learned about Ellen's sleepwalking.

"I feel so sorry for her. She undoubtedly doesn't

remember dressing up or traveling all over the house. All the tragedies the woman's endured must be responsible for her condition. Ellen admitted to me that she has dreams and sometimes wakes up more tired than when she went to bed. I think we should alert Dr. Hadley."

"Not before talking over her condition with Jonathan. There may be ramifications that we aren't aware of."

"I suppose you're right."

"Jonathan's another one under this roof who is carrying an emotional load. As acting senior member of the Langdon family, handling the scandal of Timothy's violent end will be another burden on his shoulders."

"How did Philip and Fontaine react?"

"Both of them readily expressed satisfaction that the no-account social climber got what he deserved. No love lost there. They blame Timothy for Pamela's drug addiction. If you can believe the family, she'd been clean before she became romantically involved with him. Because of Timothy's ironclad alibi of being at the yacht party when she died, I don't think the authorities looked too closely at him. I'm going to spend some time on the mainland tomorrow investigating on my own. I'll see if I can pick up anything incriminating on Kent Brenden." Then he impulsively asked, "Would you like to run over with me? Do a little shopping or something?"

She shook her head. "Can't. I worked hard today getting everything packed. Tomorrow I'll be taking care of the final preparations for shipping." She paused. "I've made my plane reservations for San Francisco the following day."

His heart sank. "Not so soon!"

"It's better that way."

"No, it isn't!" he protested. "We've got too much to say to each other. Honey, I've really dropped the ball all the way around. You can't run off and leave me without giving me the chance to explain." He put a finger over her lips when she started to argue. "I'll come back early tomorrow afternoon and we'll go for a walk and talk." He knew better than to arrange anything that wasn't extremely casual and nonthreatening.

She withdrew her hand from his. "All right, but I'm warning you, I'm not very good at goodbyes." She added in a strained voice, "Especially one like this."

They walked out of the library together. He might have kissed her good night if they hadn't seen Jonathan watching them from the door of the sitting room.

"See you tomorrow," Brad said as he turned away and headed down the hall to the front door.

Ashley pretended not to see Jonathan and hurried up the main staircase. She didn't want him asking her what they'd been talking about in the library. Tomorrow would be her last day in the house, and she was more than ready to put the tragedies of the Langdon family behind her.

THE NEXT AFTERNOON, Ashley had the entire collection ready for pickup and had alerted the auction company to arrange for the shipping of the heavily insured vintage clothes and accessories. She felt as if she'd run a marathon and just crossed the finished line. Satisfied that she'd fulfilled Lorrie's commitment to the job, Ashley did her best to ignore a persistent sense of loss. After tomorrow, she'd leave the island and Brad behind. Her emotions were in tatters.

Never being one to lie to herself, she knew putting a continent between them wasn't going to erase the heartache. It would be better to leave without seeing him again. Why in the world had she agreed to spend the last afternoon with him? It was pure stupidity to torture herself with a love that had been doomed from the beginning.

She telephoned her business in San Francisco. Kate Delawney answered. "Hollywood Boutique. How may I help you?"

"You can put out the welcome mat," Ashley answered with a smile in her voice.

"Ashley! What good news!"

"I'm finished here and taking a flight back tomorrow afternoon."

"That's wonderful. Do you want someone to pick you up at the airport?"

"No, I'll take a taxi directly to the shop."

"Wait 'til you hear the good news I have for you," Kate bubbled excitedly. "You're not going to believe it."

"Tell me now. I could use some good news."

"The west coast outlets you've been working on came through—Seattle, Los Angeles, Monterey and San Diego. Their initial orders are more than we have in stock. I don't know how we can possibly fill them."

"We'll bring in additional staff," Ashley said quickly. "Get the applications of possible new staff ready for me.

And a million thanks, Kate. You don't know what a blessing you are."

As they chatted for a few more minutes about business, Ashley realized how much she'd missed the day-to-day challenges. It would be great getting back to work—*wouldn't it?*

After she'd hung up, she quickly dialed Ted and Amy's house. She wanted to make sure her sister wouldn't be worrying about anything being left unfinished.

"Lorrie and I were just having tea," Amy said when she answered. "Wish you were here to join us, Ashley."

"I will be shortly."

"Wonderful. Here's Lorrie."

Ashley quickly told her sister she could relax. "I've finished the assignment and I'm confident the auction house will be satisfied and honor your contract with them."

"I owe you a big one, Sis," she said with an audible catch in her throat. "You really came through for me."

"That's what big sisters are for," Ashley responded lightly. "How's your health?"

"Pretty much back to normal. In fact, I'm feeling guilty about lying around. I'm ready to get back to work." She lowered her voice. "How are things going with you?"

"What do you mean?" Ashley stalled.

"As if you didn't know, Sis. Come on, give. What about you and that handsome policeman?"

"I'm afraid that's already pretty much history."

"From the sound of your voice, I can tell you're not happy about it. What happened? Did he already have someone else?"

"No, not at all," she answered quickly. "Brad...Brad loves me, and I love him, but..."

"But what for heaven's sake?"

"Simply put, we're too incompatible for a serious relationship. Brad's life and career is on the island."

"Hell's bells!" Lorrie swore. "Policemen are needed all over the place. Why can't he transfer?"

"Because the island is his life. It's a part of him and he's content to live here the rest of his life. I couldn't bear it for even a few months out of the year."

"Oh, that's a tough one."

"Yes, it's an impasse. I can't wait to get back to California and my business. I'm flying out tomorrow."

They talked for a few more minutes. After Ashley hung up, shc madc hcr way upstairs to Jonathan's office. The door was partially open and she gave a light knock as she peered in. He was sitting motionless behind his desk and visibly stiffened when he saw her.

"May I come in?"

He nodded but didn't get to his feet in his usual polite manner. He clasped his hands on the desk and waited for her to speak. Ashley thought he'd visibly aged since last evening when he'd heard about the ugly cemetery discovery.

"I just wanted to tell you that the auction company will be arranging for shipment of the collection," Ashley said, remaining standing. "Everything has been inventoried and packed."

"Well, I guess that's it, then. Maybe someone will get some pleasure out of the things my wife enjoyed so much," he said as he looked beyond Ashley to the portrait of Samantha on the far wall.

"I'm sure the collection will be well-received. The monetary value should be substantial."

He shrugged as if his thoughts were too weighted to think about dollars and cents.

"I'll be leaving tomorrow and returning to San Francisco. I talked to Lorrie a few minutes ago and I know everyone will be happy to know she has fully recovered."

Except for the one who tried to kill her!

BRAD HAD SAID he'd pick her up about four o'clock. She wore her knit pants suit with a soft blue scarf for accent. She was waiting on the front veranda when she glimpsed the patrol car through the canopy of trees. She made her way to the front step when he pulled up.

At first, she thought her eyes were deceiving her.

Deputy Hunskut was driving.

The deputy quickly got out and came around the car. "Brad got tied up and asked me to save him the time of driving up here and picking you up. I don't mind chauffeuring a pretty lady at all," he told her, smiling.

As he gallantly opened the door for her, she fought the temptation to change her mind about going. She hated farewells especially one she'd have to live with forever.

"When does he think he'll be free?"

"He called and said he'd be heading back from the mainland shortly. He thought you'd rather wait for him at his house than here."

As she got in the car, something about this arrangement raised a warning flag. Brad had said they would take a walk and talk. More than ever, she needed a neutral environment to keep her feelings under control.

"I hear you're about ready to leave us?" Bill said.

"Tomorrow."

"That's too bad. I guess you'll be back before too long?"

Ashley ignored the question in his tone and just offered some benign remark about the clearing weather. As they passed Dr. Hadley's home, Bill slowed down and waved. The doctor nodded and gave Ashley a broad smile as if he knew she was headed for a rendezvous with Brad.

As the deputy turned into Brad's driveway, she was tempted to tell him to take her back to the Langdons'. Just looking at the house taunted her with memories of their passionate lovemaking.

"The door's unlocked and Brad said you might want to take Rusty for a walk while you waited."

Good, she thought in relief. She wouldn't have to wait in the house. What she needed was a hearty walk to maintain her emotional balance. She was already feeling a deep sense of loss. He'd made her feel truly alive and desirable for the first time in her life. Brad had been a tender lover, gentle and yet in command. She cursed the fates that had put them on such divergent paths.

"If I don't see you again before you leave, have a safe trip," Bill told her. "My mother sends her best, too."

"Thank you. Tell her I'd love to have a copy of her cemetery article when it comes out."

Rusty gave her an ecstatic welcome as she let him out of the dog run. Bounding around her and wagging his tail, the dog offered her warm, sloppy kisses.

"How about a walk, fellow?"

Rusty seemed to understand perfectly. He bounded around the house and down a path leading to the rocky beach below. As Ashley followed him, she drew in deep breaths of the fresh salty air.

An incoming tide was narrowing the shore as Rusty sniffed his way along the tumbled rocks, investigating the smorgasbord of smells. When he scrambled on top of a pile of gray rocks and began barking furiously at something out in the water, Ashley couldn't see what was causing all the ruckus.

"Rusty! Rusty! Get back here."

When he wouldn't come, she gingerly climbed up on the rocks to see what he was having such a fit about. As she braced herself on the rugged rocks, she looked out into the water and saw that three black seals were lounging on some ocean rocks. One of them slithered into the water and seemed headed in their direction. When Rusty made a move to scoot down and into the water, Ashley tried to grab his collar.

She lost her balance! Stones loosened by the recent storm slipped out from under her feet. They pelted down on top of her as she tumbled down the rocky incline to the edge of the water. When she sat up, she felt a burning pain in the calf of one leg. Quickly she lifted her pants leg and saw blood oozing out of a deep, jagged cut.

"Damn," she swore.

She struggled to her feet and gritted her teeth against the pain as she limped her way along the beach, and up the steep path to the house. Rusty seemed to know the walk was over and trotted obediently at her heels.

Sweat beaded on her forehead as she let herself inside and headed for the bathroom. She tried to stop the bleeding as best she could by tying her scarf around the cut but she knew it was going to need stitches. She remembered that the deputy had waved to Dr. Hadley as they drove past, so she knew he was home. The only sensible thing to do was to hobble to his house and ask him to tend the wound.

She should have shut Rusty up before she left, but she didn't think about it until he started running way ahead of her. As far as she knew, Brad only took him for runs on the beach. He would be furious if the dog got away.

"Rusty, come back!" she yelled.

At the sound of her voice, he stopped momentarily, wagged his tail, and then headed out again. He was sniffing around the doctor's yard when she finally hobbled to the front steps of the house. Blood had already soaked the scarf she'd tied around the wound.

Rusty suddenly appeared and bounded up the steps ahead of her. With the aid of a guard rail, she mounted the five wooden steps. The front door was open and Ashley could see an empty room through the screen. A welcoming sign reading Come In And Be Seated was posted on the door frame.

As she opened the screen door, she heard a bell ringing somewhere in the depths of the house. She was tempted to give a demanding cry for immediate help but decided against embarrassing herself with all the dramatics.

She stepped inside, with the dog at her heels.

The next instant, all hell broke loose.

Stiff-legged and hissing, a huge cat suddenly rose in one of the chairs in the waiting room. Rusty went berserk!

In a split second, the dog was after the cat as it leapt from the chair onto the doctor's desk. Rusty followed, scattering papers and books in every direction. The cat jumped from the desk to the top of a filing cabinet.

"Rusty! No. No. Down! Down!" she ordered as the dog rose high enough on his hind legs to almost reach the cowering cat.

With the dog barking and snapping at him, the cat jumped from the top of the cabinet onto an adjoining wall shelf which instantly came crashing down with the added weight.

Ashley was standing close enough to the screen door to fling it open as the cat hit the floor and became a flash of black fur as it bounded out of the house. Before Ashley could get the door closed again, Rusty was in hot pursuit.

Ashley limped over to a chair and dropped down in it.

"Dr. Hadley! Dr. Hadley!" she called as loudly as she could. In all the commotion, there was still no sign of the doctor. When she heard the faint closing of a door somewhere at the back of the house, she guessed he must have been outside. "I need help!"

The floor was littered with papers, books and objects

that had been on the wall shelf when it fell. Some animal figures were broken, and a ceramic box was now a pile of jagged shards.

As she stared at the broken objects, she suddenly stiffened.

Forgetting all about her bleeding leg, she leaned over and picked up a piece of recognizable jewelry lying among the broken pieces of the shattered box. As she held it in her hand, she stopped breathing.

The missing necklace from Lorrie's inventory!

With trembling fingers, she carefully opened the locket. Two cameo pictures were inside. One of them was a smiling, youthful Samantha, easily recognizable from several pictures Ashley had seen in the house. The opposite photo was of neither Jonathan Langdon nor Philip Langdon but of another young, handsome young man.

James Hadley, MD.

Bits and pieces of the truth hit her with dynamic revelation. Her thoughts whirled like an off-center gyroscope. Too late, she sensed a presence behind her.

Before she could move, a strong arm came around her and pinned her back in the chair. She glimpsed the doctor's face as a needle plunged into her neck.

"No…no…please, no!" Her cries echoed in her ears as her body disintegrated into a thousand floating pieces.

Chapter Fifteen

Brad spent more time than he'd planned at the state medical examiner's office in Portland. During his years as a police officer on the mainland, he'd had contact with a lot of the personnel at the forensic laboratory. Cutting up dead bodies was not high on his list of enviable jobs, and he had a lot of respect for the work the forensics staff did.

"What do you have for me, Dr. McBride?" Brad asked a bespectacled little man who had spent thirty years of his life finding answers hidden in the remains of the deceased. Brad was confident he could trust this tenacious and talented man.

"You were right about the identity, Brad. It's Timothy Templeton. We secured hospital X-rays taken a few years ago of a mended shoulder injury of the young man. I can show you on the skeleton how they match."

"No need," Brad said, declining the offer. "What killed him?"

McBride shook his head. "I can't tell you right off.

Because of the decomposition of the body, we'll have to conduct more tests, but I can tell you what didn't." McBride shoved his glasses back on his rather pointed nose. "There's no evidence of trauma to the skeleton, such as blows or bullets. My guess is poison or a fatal injection of some kind. After several years of decomposition, we're limited in the kind of reliable tests that we can do."

"I can't find any record of Timothy having been seen anywhere after Pamela Langdon's death. Did you do the autopsy on her?"

McBride nodded. "We doubled-checked everything on that one. Old Man Langdon was really breathing down our necks. Our analysis showed a lethal combination of drugs and alcohol. As far as we could tell, she did it to herself."

"That's what the police decided, too."

"I remember one unusual thing," he said, lowering his voice. "I didn't say anything about it to anyone at the time. It wasn't relative to the investigation."

"What was that?"

"I inadvertently discovered, through medical backgrounds on the family, that Pamela Langdon didn't have the same blood type as either Samantha or Jonathan. The girl was Type O while Samantha was Type A and Jonathan is Type AB."

"What does that mean?"

"Maybe nothing. Sometimes it happens that the child has a different blood type than either parent, but it's rare. So I'd have to question it."

Brad slowly let out his breath. "I think you're on to something, Doc."

McBride nodded. "Since the mother and daughter are both dead, I guess it doesn't matter much."

"I'm not so sure."

All the way back to the island, Brad pondered what this new development might mean. He doubted that the Langdon family would consider adoption. The alternative seemed more probable. Samantha Langdon could have had a lover who was the father of her child!

Checking the blood types of any man in Samantha's life about the time she got pregnant might reveal the one that matched Pamela's.

His deputy had left the police car at the wharf and Brad's mind was whirling with ways to pursue this new line of investigation as he drove home. As he passed Dr. Hadley's house, Brad slowed the car. If anyone knew about the inconsistencies in the Langdon bloodline, it would have to be Dr. Hadley.

When Brad saw the doctor coming up the path from the beach, he impulsively braked and pulled into the driveway. Even though he knew Ashley was waiting, his investigative juices were at an all-time high.

He got out of the car and headed around the house to the backyard. Since Hadley had been pushing a wheelbarrow, Brad decided he must have been dumping some debris or rocks from his garden onto the rugged beach below. The doctor was putting the wheelbarrow into a walk-in shed and throwing a canvas over it when Brad came around the corner of the house.

"Have you got a minute, Doc?" Brad called to him.

As he turned around, Hadley's face was flush and sweat beaded on his forehead. "What is it?"

"Just a couple of questions."

"I'm afraid they'll have to wait," he answered curtly. "I have several calls I have to make as soon I clean up and get a bite to eat. Let's make it first thing in the morning, Officer."

Hadley was obviously tired, uptight and irritable. No wonder, Brad thought. The storm had put an extra burden on the doctor's time and energy.

"Sure, Doc. Tomorrow will be soon enough."

"Good. See you then." Hadley nodded and then quickly walked across the yard and disappeared through thc back door of his house.

Brad glanced at his watch. He was really late. If his deputy had picked Ashley up on time, she'd really be tired of waiting.

Brad was just opening the car door to get in when he heard a rushing noise behind him. He swung around.

"What in the—"

He couldn't believe his eyes when he saw Rusty racing up the driveway toward the car. Without waiting for an invitation, Rusty jumped into the middle of the front seat and sat there, panting and slobbering, obviously worn out from some kind of chase.

Brad didn't know whether to scold or hug the dog. He'd always been careful not to let Rusty run around freely. When they went for walks, it was along the shoreline. "Did Ashley let you out? I'll have to have a talk with her, won't I?"

Even as he chided the dog, he knew there wouldn't be any purpose in telling her anything. This would be the last time she'd be at his house waiting for him.

Tomorrow she'd be gone.

A RISING SURF roared in her ears. Surrounded by dirt and rock walls, she fought to focus her heavy-lidded eyes. Fading sunlight coming through a jagged opening between huge boulders gave her a glimpse of the swelling ocean beyond. The ground was wet and cold and sent a bone-deep chill through her body as she lay there motionless.

This wasn't happening! It was a nightmare. A terrifying dream. Wake up! Wake up!

Even as she fought the horror of her surroundings, she knew she wasn't dreaming. She was awake. Disjointed thoughts slowly began to take shape. Like the jagged pieces of a puzzle, they came together. She remembered!

Dr. Hadley! The necklace! The photos!

She had to tell Brad! He would know how to put it all together. A sharp urgency shot through her. Her fingers dug feebly into the moist, slimy ground as she tried to move—and couldn't. There were no ropes or bonds preventing her from getting up. The horrible truth swept over her.

Dear God, no!

Whatever drug Hadley had given her had affected her muscles. Her arms and legs were unresponsive. She could only move her head slightly to one side.

The sound of an incoming tide was like a death knell. She was as helpless as if she were already buried in her watery grave. Slowly and relentlessly the water began to spread wider and wider into the cave. Higher and higher…

Rising seawater slowly covered Ashley's feet and puddled all around her chilled flesh. The cut in her leg smarted from the salty water and the cloth she had wrapped around it had dropped off. She didn't know how much blood she had lost. She desperately struggled to move her inert body but a little movement of her head and her fingers was the only response. Her nostrils were filled with the pungent odors of decaying seaweed and dank driftwood.

Waves of unconsciousness only heightened her terror as she was repeatedly thrust back into an awareness of lingering death. Her ears were filled with the roar of a rising surf coming closer and closer. The incoming tide would inevitably fill the cavern and sweep her body out to sea. Her mind refused to comprehend why a twisted fate had brought her to this end.

BRAD SAW Ashley's sweater on one of the chairs as soon as he and Rusty came through the kitchen into the house.

Good, at least she'd waited.

"Sorry I'm late but I—" He stopped when he saw that the living room was empty.

Maybe she was sitting on the back patio. He quickly went outside and checked, but there wasn't any sign that she might have sat there waiting for him.

More than anything, Rusty's calm behavior as he

tagged along at Brad's heels verified that Ashley wasn't in the house. The dog always made a complete pest of himself when there was anyone around.

Ashley must have gotten tired of waiting! The Langdon compound was less than a mile's walk. When he didn't show, she'd probably left in a huff, forgetting her sweater.

All the things he'd wanted to say to her were a hollow mockery. He'd even been ready to promise he'd put his police work on the back burner to spend more time with her if she'd stay. The truth was, he had no real life separate from his work and the timing would always be bad. How could he plead with her to give their love a chance when she'd end up resenting him for ruining her life? No, it was better this way. Better to let her leave tomorrow without creating another painful scene between them.

He dropped down on the living room couch and the dog jumped up beside him. Brad scratched Rusty head and said, "It's just you and me, fellow."

He must have sat there ten minutes before he noticed the glass door was slightly open.

He sat up. Had Ashley left it open? She could have decided to take a walk while she was waiting and let Rusty out.

His thoughts came to a screeching halt. Maybe the dog had gotten away from her and gone off on his own? That would explain Rusty's runaway appearance at the doctor's house. Maybe Ashley was still out hunting for him!

Brad was on his feet and out the door in an instant.

From his backyard, he had a good view of the shoreline below the house. Looking in both directions, he failed to see her anywhere along the rugged shore. The beach had narrowed with the incoming tide and as deep white-foamed surf began to assault the shoreline, it would soon completely disappear.

He raced down to the water and headed for the best view of the surrounding terrain. He quickly climbed to the top of the granite boulders, and let his eyes travel in every direction. No sign of her slender figure anywhere.

He must have jumped to the wrong conclusion, Brad told himself. Somehow Rusty had gotten out and run away. Disappointed, he returned to the house with muddy boots and hands and went into the bathroom to clean up.

"What in the—"

He froze in the doorway when he saw a bloody towel lying on the floor and a mound of bloody tissues stuffed in the wastepaper basket.

Ashley! What had happened? Had someone attacked her? Left her here, bleeding? Had she injured herself? How badly was she hurt?

Where was she now?

She didn't have a car. Bill had brought her to the house. If she'd hurt herself, she might have called him to take her to the doctor.

Doctor?

He'd just been at Dr. Hadley's house. And so had Rusty! Maybe Rusty had followed her there. Had the doctor treated Ashley and not said anything about it? But why wouldn't he? Dr. Hadley could have treated

Ashley and called the Langdons for someone to pick her up. He quickly called the doctor's house, but the line was busy.

"No, you stay here," he ordered as he shut the dog inside. He didn't bother with the car. His long legs covered the ground between the two properties at a run. The sight of the bloody bathroom had sent a burst of adrenaline coursing through him.

A double garage was attached to Hadley's house, but the doors were shut. He couldn't tell if the doctor's car was still there. Brad's chest tightened. Trying to locate Dr. Hadley could waste valuable time.

Brad bounded up the porch steps and pounded on the front door.

"Hadley! Open up!"

No answer. No hint of movement inside. Maybe he was in the back of the house. Brad sprinted around to the rear door. No answer.

The backyard was empty. Maybe he was still making trips down to the shore. Brad scanned the rocky beach below. No sign of him. The tide was already coming in.

As Brad turned back toward the house, he saw that the door to the walk-in shed was open and wondered if Hadley had meant to leave it open. There was nothing in it but tools, gardening supplies, and the wheelbarrow Hadley had been using earlier. The canvas he'd thrown over it hung down one side and as Brad's trained eyes swept over it, they registered a tiny bright splotch on one corner. He reached for the canvas and jerked it up.

Blood!

The inside of the wheelbarrow was smeared with it.

An instant replay shot through Brad's mind.

Hadley coming up the beach path!

Pushing the wheelbarrow!

Sweating and ill at ease!

Fresh blood.

Brad didn't waste a split second trying to understand the how or why. He raced down the path to the shoreline.

Faint impressions of the wheelbarrow's tires in the wet sand were rapidly being washed away. He followed them to an outcropping of tumbled boulders. Then they disappeared.

A bewildering mass of granite slabs and underground caverns lay ahead.

Brad had almost missed the jagged opening between the slanting granite boulders forming the low-ceilinged cave. He'd passed it on his first hurried search.

As the rising tide swept in, the wheelbarrow tracks had been washed away. Brad couldn't tell when they ended or how much farther Hadley had gone after all the tracks had disappeared. Tumbled rocks and fallen earth made the side of the high bank an impossible climb.

Hadley wasn't muscular enough to have carried her very far.

He spun on his water-logged boots and quickly backtracked. He looked for any opening in the rocks and bank that was wide enough for a human body to squeeze through.

If the fading sun hadn't hit the opening just right, he

might have missed the narrow passage through the tumbled boulders. Water was already up to his ankles when he splashed his way into a shadowy cavern.

He blinked rapidly to clear his vision. When he saw a dark shape on the water-logged ground, he couldn't believe it was really her until he bent over her crumpled body.

"Ashley..." he choked as he gathered her close. When he felt the blessed rise and fall of her chest, his eyes were suddenly moist with emotion.

She was alive!

He quickly lifted her up and as the fading sunlight hit her face, she seemed to smile. He splashed through the swelling tide and carried her tenderly up the path to Hadley's house.

He was prepared to break a window to get in, but the back door was unlocked.

Once inside the house, he carried her muddy, drenched body into the nearest bedroom and put her on the bed. Her pant leg was muddy, bloody, and wet.

"It's all right. You're safe now."

Her eyelashes fluttered and then lay still upon her bleached skin. She was like a rag doll in his hands as he stripped off the wet and muddy clothes and cleaned her wound. Then he wrapped her in blankets for warmth.

Grabbing the telephone sitting on a nightstand, he dialed an emergency number on the mainland.

His call was answered immediately. "Helicopter Medical Services."

"Officer Taylor on Greystone," he barked. "Red alert.

Send a chopper immediately. A young woman. Life-threatening condition."

"You got it, Brad," a woman replied.

He called Bill and ordered, "Ashley's hurt. I've got a helicopter coming to the pad. Meet us there!"

"Yes, sir." His deputy knew better than to delay by asking questions.

He hung up and ran out to the garage. Thank heavens the emergency van they kept at the doctor's house was ready and waiting. Using his keys, Brad opened up the back and put the stretcher in the correct position to handle Ashley's body when he brought her out. Then he hurried back into the house.

She was still motionless and unconscious when he lifted her up from the bed. He had always prided himself on controlling his emotions, but as he held her blanket-wrapped body in his arms, she looked so fragile, so vulnerable, so damn helpless, that an all-consuming rage rose in him.

I'll kill him. I'll kill the bastard!

Chapter Sixteen

Bill was already at the baseball field when Brad pulled in with the ambulance. When the deputy saw Ashley's still form on the stretcher, he swore, "What the hell happened?"

Angrily, Brad told him where he'd found Ashley and the doctor's part in it.

"I can't believe it! Hadley? Why—?"

"Ashley must have posed a threat, or learned something that could incriminate him. While I wait for the ambulance, get down to the pier and check on Hadley's boat. My guess is he won't stick around long. He won't want to chance someone tying him to Ashley's disappearance. We need to get him before he leaves the island. Do what you have to do to detain him."

"You got it!"

The pier was only a short distance away from the playing field where the helicopter would land. Brad wasn't about to leave Ashley until he put her in the care of the paramedics.

He gently brushed back her damp hair and when he cradled her hand in his, he was startled as her fingers tightened slightly. Her eyes slowly opened and focused on his face.

"Hang in there, sweetheart. Help is on the way." Even as he spoke, he heard the whirling sound of a helicopter and dirt kicking up on the playing field.

As soon as the helicopter landed, two paramedics, a man and woman, emerged with a stretcher and headed for the ambulance.

"What do we have here?" the man asked as he looked down at Ashley's colorless face and motionless body.

Brad briefed them as much as he could, but he was at a loss as to what Hadley had done to her before he dumped her in the cavern.

"Okay, we'll take it from here."

Brad stayed out of the way as the paramedics quickly began their routine and readied her for the emergency flight.

When they were ready to lift her into the helicopter, Brad kissed her on the cheek and promised, "I'll come to the hospital as soon as I can."

After I've arrested the bastard who did this to you!

As soon as the helicopter had disappeared into the twilight, Brad quickly drove the ambulance down to the pier.

Before he could get out of the car, Bill ran to meet him. From his deputy's expression, Brad knew the news wasn't good.

"Hadley's boat's gone!"

Brad swore under his breath. "Anybody see him leave?"

"Yeah, a couple of guys who were just coming in with their lobster catch. About ten minutes ago. Hadley got in his boat and headed north."

"North?"

"That's what they said."

"Is the patrol boat gassed up and ready?"

"Yes, sir. Filled it up this morning."

"Okay, let's go."

The patrol boat sent a high white foam tail into the air as Brad headed north at a high speed. Hadley must have decided going to the mainland was too risky, Brad reasoned. Going north, the doctor would leave U.S. waters behind, and his chances of disappearing would undoubtedly be better if he made it into Canada.

"We'd better catch him before dark," Bill said as he searched the waters ahead. There were literally hundreds of places along the eastern seaboard where a boat could disappear for days.

Traffic had thinned out considerably in just a matter of minutes. They passed fewer and fewer boats the farther north they went, which made it easier to identify the remaining ones heading up the coast to Nova Scotia and beyond.

Brad was beginning to wonder if Hadley had already pulled to the shore and was no longer on the water when Bill shouted and pointed, "Straight ahead. There he is!"

The doctor's small fishing boat was easily recognizable. Everyone on the island had seen him coming and going in it. Brad's hands tightened fiercely on the wheel. As the distance between them lessened, Brad maneuvered the patrol boat into a position so that it was running parallel with Hadley's boat.

The doctor must have realized what was happening and opened the throttle because the small boat suddenly jumped forward at a dangerous speed.

Brad instantly responded. The larger and heavier patrol boat kept abreast of the smaller craft as it tried to get away.

As the two boats raced side by side, they could see Hadley's hunched figure bent over the wheel.

Bill grabbed a megaphone and yelled, "Cut your motor! Now!"

Hadley ignored the order.

Brad dangerously narrowed the distance between the two racing boats, bringing them closer together. Fearing the patrol boat was going to ram him, Hadley gave his boat a sudden turn.

The result was disaster!

The high speed and jerky movement brought the small boat up on its side. For an electrifying moment, it wavered, slicing through the water at a pitched angle. Then the boat flipped over!

Brad was able to keep from crashing into the capsized boat as the patrol boat raced by it. Then, as quickly as he could, he cut his speed, turned around and came to the place where Hadley's boat was slowly sinking out of sight.

"Do you see him?" Bill asked, ready to throw a life preserver.

Brad shook his head. The lights of the patrol boat played over the water, but debris was the only thing coming to the surface as the small boat disappeared. They were miles from any shore. If Hadley had survived and made it to the surface, Brad was confident they would have seen him.

As the minutes passed, the moon came up and spread a patina of flickering light across the water. Finally Brad said, "Well, I guess that's it. I'll radio the coast guard and report the drowning."

Justice had been served after all. James Hadley, MD, had met the watery death he'd planned for Ashley.

ASHLEY WAS still in intensive care the next morning when Brad was allowed to see her. One of the nurses had told her that he'd had been at the hospital all night. When Brad came into the room, he was unshaven, with dark lines under his eyes and worried creases around his mouth.

"You look awful," she told him.

His expression was one of astonishment and visible relief. "No need to ask if you're feeling better. They didn't tell me you're already back to your usual feisty self."

"Not quite," she admitted with a wan smile. "But I can move now."

"Terrific." He bent over and kissed her. "You're amazing. The last time I saw you—"

"The paralysis was temporary," she told him quickly. She explained how her muscles had slowly began to respond as the drug in her body lost its effect. "I'll have some physical therapy to make sure all my nerves are functioning before they release me."

"Then all is well."

A rising swell of anger made her ask bluntly, "Did you get him?"

"Yes."

The hardness in his eyes made her gasp, "Did you… did you kill him?"

"No. He drowned and saved me the trouble."

Briefly he told her about the chase and what had happened. "I'm trying to understand exactly what Hadley's role was in all this. I need you to tell me exactly what happened."

She shuddered, not wanting to relive the terror again. More than anything, she wanted to forget those torturous hours, when she was alone and helpless. Would she ever forget the sound of the waves coming closer and closer?

"I'm sorry but I have to know."

She swallowed hard and then she told him how she hurt her leg and had gone to Hadley's house to have him look at it. She described the fracas between Rusty and the cat. Brad's eyes widened when she told him about finding the necklace and seeing young Dr. Hadley's picture opposite Samantha's in the locket.

"He must have stopped in the workroom when he was in the house tending Clayton and spied the necklace in the pile of jewelry Lorrie was adding to the inventory," Ashley speculated. "And thinking Lorrie had already seen his picture in the locket he..." Her voice faltered.

"He tried to silence her," Brad finished. "Yes, that must have been the way it happened. Hadley couldn't have his identity as Samantha's lover revealed to the Langdons." Brad whistled softly. "I need to check his blood type."

"Whatever for? You've lost me. What does that have to do with anything?"

"Maybe plenty if the match proves Hadley was the father of Samantha's daughter, Pamela."

Ashley's head was already swimming with too many unanswered questions. She was glad Brad was the one who had to make sense of it all. She didn't want to know any more about the tangled lives of the Langdon family. As far as she was concerned, if she never heard the name Langdon again, it would be too soon.

Brad leaned down and kissed her gently on the forehead. "You're one brave woman." His voice thickened. "And I love you more than I thought I could ever love anyone."

She wanted to declare her feelings for him, but the words wouldn't come. What good would it do to confess she felt the same way about him? Why declare a love that was doomed from the beginning? After what had happened, she couldn't wait to leave and never set foot on his beloved island again.

THAT AFTERNOON, Brad headed out in the patrol boat for Minnequa Island. He wanted to talk with Mary Sandrow. News about the doctor's drowning had already been circulating on the mainland. He wondered if Mary had heard about Hadley's demise. One look at her haggard face when she opened the door gave him the answer. The hatred in her eyes warned him that if she'd had a gun, she might have shot him then and there.

"It's over, Mary," he said in a firm, official tone. "We need to talk. The best thing you can do now is come clean and avoid any legal prosecution."

"I haven't done a damn thing but keep my mouth shut."

"A judge might consider that a clear case of blackmail. You really don't have much choice, Mary. Everything about Samantha and Hadley is going to come out. Medical tests will prove he was Pamela's father."

The woman seemed to visibly shrink in front of his eyes. She lowered her head, her thick shoulders slumped, and her arms fell listlessly to her sides.

"I know the secrets you've been keeping for all these years, Mary. Why don't you explain everything to me and I promise to help you if I can?"

She turned slowly away from the door and Brad followed her as she shuffled down the hall to the sitting room. Without speaking she sat down in a large, padded chair. A box of tissues were within reach on a nearby table, and a pile of them were crumpled up in a heap. She took one, dabbed her eyes and blew her nose without speaking.

Brad almost felt sorry for her. Even though Mary Sandrow been paid well for her silence, he wondered if money had ever been enough to compensate for the loss of the young woman and her baby whom she had loved so deeply.

When she began to talk, it was as if dammed-up emotions had been seeking release all these years. Brad was looking for verification of what he already knew and she gave it to him.

Samantha and James Hadley had begun their affair when he was a successful New York physician and came to the island for his summer vacations.

"She was crazy about him but wouldn't divorce Jonathan." Mary sighed. "Samantha liked the Langdon money and prestige too much. Hadley would fly to Portland as often as possible, and they would rendezvous on the mainland."

"What about the night of the accident?"

Mary nodded. Hadley been in the car with Samantha when it went off the road into the water. "The crash killed her, but he was uninjured. More than anything, he wanted to protect her good name. Somehow, he managed to get away from the scene before the crash was reported."

"Did he know Pamela was his child?"

Mary dabbed at her eyes. "Yes. I guess he did a blood test or something. They kept it all secret. Samantha wanted Pamela to enjoy the Langdon money and prestige. Hadley did, too. He was crazy about Pamela.

They became good friends as she was growing up and she was the reason he retired early and came back to the island to live when she was a young lady. When he saw she was into drugs and drinking, he almost had her convinced to give up that lifestyle." Her mouth tightened. "That's when Timothy Templeton came on the scene. The doctor blamed him for Pamela's death. I've never seen anyone so consumed with rage. He threatened to kill him."

Mary obviously didn't know Hadley had carried out his threat. "Mary, did you call Hadley and tell him I had made an appointment to come and talk with you?"

She nodded. "He made me promise to always tell him if anyone was snooping around, asking questions."

"And what did he say when you told him?"

"Nothing much. He said for me not to worry, that he'd take care of it."

He almost did, Brad said under his breath.

"What's going to happen now?" Mary asked him in a frightened voice. "I've told you everything. You have to protect me against the Langdons. They'll want revenge for all the secrets I've been keeping."

"They have too many secrets of their own to worry about," Brad reassured her. "If I were you, I'd hold fast and see what happens."

"I won't be getting any more money from Dr. Hadley?"

"I'm afraid not."

He left her hunched in her chair, staring at the floor and wiping at her eyes.

WHEN BRAD GOT BACK to the island, he was pleased Bill had left the patrol car at the pier. There were a couple of stops he wanted to make right away.

He drove directly to Hadley's house. He'd used the back door when carrying Ashley out to the ambulance, but the front door was unlocked and when he went in, he saw the mess Ashley had described. She'd told him she'd picked up the necklace and had dropped it when Hadley attacked her. He didn't see any sign of it on the floor and had decided the doctor must have taken it. But then he glimpsed a tiny chain almost hidden in a chair cushion. It must have slipped down in the chair when Hadley attacked her. Apparently, he was too busy disposing of her to worry about finding it.

Brad went through the house, out the back door and then headed to the shed again. He walked past the bloody wheelbarrow and canvas, and began searching some boxes piled in the corner. In a large one on the bottom, he found what he was looking for.

Everything needed to put together a lethal firebomb.

Satisfied that an official team of investigators would find all the evidence they needed to know the truth, he headed home, certain that Bill had taken care of Rusty last night and this morning. His deputy loved the dog as if he belonged to him.

PHYSICALLY, Ashley bounced back in only a couple of days. But the emotional aftermath of everything that had happened took its toll.

Even though the Langdons did everything they could

to suppress publicity, it was a losing battle. Having been promised immunity, Mary Sandrow was ready and willing to tell all. Ironically, the press played her up as a loyal servant and confidante of the idle rich who had kept her secrets out of loyalty and not for money. She'd wisely warned Hadley that she'd left a written record of everything to become public if something happened to her.

Brad did his best to protect Ashley's identity and arranged for her to give her testimony in private.

"I can't promise that you won't be called upon at a later date," he warned her. "This is too hot of a story for the media to let it rest. Don't talk on the phone to anyone and don't admit any visitors who you don't know.

"I think you should leave as soon as possible," he told her as if she were some kind of burden to him.

It did no good to remind herself of the pressure he was under. There was no evidence of the passionate love that had been between them.

"Yes, I'll make reservations."

"As early as in the morning. Or even the red-eye flight tonight if you feel up to it," he insisted.

"Tonight," she said in a tremulous voice.

HE PICKED her up at midnight and drove her to the airport. As a spattering of rain hit the windshield and strong gusts of wind buffeted the car, it seemed to Ashley that even the elements were anxious to see her go. She felt alone and strangely lost.

Even the warmth of the car and Brad's strong body sitting close to her offered no reassurance. She was leaving with even less than she'd brought on her arrival. Nothing in the world would have made her return to the Langdon compound to claim her belongings.

He didn't say anything until he parked the car and turned off the engine. Then he reached for her as if trying to hold on to something fast slipping away. Her arms were around his neck and she clung to him as his lips greedily claimed hers. In that moment, she surrendered and whispered, "I can't go. I'll stay."

He instantly pulled back, shook his head and said firmly, "No, you're going now."

He didn't give her a chance to argue as they walked into the terminal in silence. He took care of everything at the ticket counter and accompanied her to the security gates.

He kissed her again, this time on her cheek, and then turned away in a poignant, wordless goodbye.

Epilogue

Christmas was only a week away and Hollywood Boutique housed in a new location was gaily decorated for the holidays. Ashley had welcomed the hectic demands of this larger store, which better accommodated a dozen women working to fill orders for an ever-increasing number of outlets. Colorful windows displayed beaded purses, scarfs, bracelets, necklaces, lapel pins and a variety of beaded garments.

"You're getting to be quite an icon in the fashion world," Lorrie teased. Her sister called every week from New York where she'd taken a position with a creative fabric designer. "Some day, I'll have to say 'I knew you when'."

Ashley laughed. "I doubt that. Anyway, I'm trying to clear up everything before you get here."

"That's what I called you about. My plans have changed and I won't be coming. I hope you'll understand." Her voice betrayed her excitement. "I've been dating somebody very special. I wasn't sure how he felt about me until now." She took a deep breath. "Last night, Michael proposed and I accepted. Can you believe it! We're going to visit his folks in Philadelphia for Christmas, to tell them the good news. I hope you understand."

"Of course, I do. It's wonderful, Loribelle," Ashley answered readily. "I didn't have any idea. Why didn't you tell me about him before now?"

Lorrie hesitated. "Because I knew how much you were hurting. It's a damn shame that you aren't the one planning a wedding."

"Don't be silly. Brad is just history."

"You're a terrible liar, Sis. Have you heard from him recently?"

"Not for a couple of months. He called me several times just after I got back, bringing me up to date on things. I owe him a lot for keeping me out of the newspapers."

"Apparently the Langdons closed up the house and moved back to New York," Lorrie said. "I saw in the paper that Clayton Langdon died."

"I know. I guess all the ugly publicity was too much for him." Ashley sighed. "Anyway, Brad called once a couple of weeks ago when I was in San Diego."

"Why didn't you call him back?"

"We don't have much to say to each other," Ashley replied and quickly changed the subject. "What kind of a wedding are you planning?"

They talked for another half hour and after they'd said goodbye, Ashley tried not to think about spending

Christmas without her sister. Through the years, they'd managed to be together for almost all of them, but Ashley knew that from now on, Lorrie would be involved more and more in her own life.

"I'd better get used to it," she told herself and forced her mind to concentrate on something else.

When Kate Delawney came into the office in the late afternoon, she informed Ashley, "There are a couple of salesmen wanting to see you. I tried to tell them to come back after the holidays, but one of them just shook his head and said he'd wait."

Ashley muttered curses as she pushed back her chair. She felt like locking the front door and sending everyone home until after Christmas.

The remaining salesman stood with his back to her. He was tall, broad-shouldered, wearing a tweed jacket that picked up the russet-brown tones in his hair. Even before he turned around, her heart had begun to race with recognition.

"Brad," she choked.

"Hi," he said, smiling. "The real salesman left. I hope you're not too disappointed."

She went into his arms, much too overcome with emotion to even answer. Many sleepless nights, she'd fantasized what she would do if he suddenly appeared; even now, when she felt the warmth of his embrace and kiss, she couldn't believe that it was really happening.

"You're here…in San Francisco."

"I can hardly believe it myself," he admitted with a

grin. "I was asked to come and take care of some other business, and—" He glanced at the women standing round, exchanging smiles and winks. "Is there some place where we can talk?"

"Yes, of course."

She led him into her office and shut the door. He kissed her again and breathlessly she motioned for him to sit down with her on a small sofa.

"What kind of business?" she asked as evenly as she could. Something other than coming to see her had brought him to the west coast. She expected him to say he was involved in some kind of law enforcement assignment.

"You're not going to believe it." He chuckled and shook his head. "But then maybe you won't be surprised at all. It was your idea, really."

"What are you talking about?"

"Remember you said I should submit some of my photographs for competition? Well, I did. Dora Hunskut told me that *Nature Trails* magazine was offering five hundred dollars to the winner of a contest they were conducting. Guess what?"

"You won?"

"I did! They're handing out the prizes this evening at their publishing company, and I have to be there."

"That's wonderful! Absolutely wonderful."

"Will you go with me?"

"You couldn't keep me away. The store closes at six. I'll be ready to go."

She was glad she kept a couple of nice outfits at the

store so she could change from her day clothes if need be for some unexpected reason.

Going out on a date with Brad Taylor was certainly unexpected.

He arrived a few minutes early and whistled when he saw her. She was wearing an ivory dress and a matching jacket fashioned with gold beaded cuffs and collar. She'd brushed her hair into a twist at the back of her neck and fastened it with a gold clip.

"I guess I'd better put on a tie." They laughed as he pulled one out of his pocket and she knotted it for him.

They had dinner at Fisherman's Wharf. Christmas lights reflecting in the nearby water and festive holiday decorations wove a magic spell as they strolled arm in arm. She fought back a lingering sadness that this would only be another painful memory when he returned to his island.

They took a taxi to the high-rise building where the *Nature Trails* magazine had their offices. Ashley could tell Brad wasn't particularly at ease as they took the elevator to the twentieth floor. She teased him about taking the stairs instead.

"I guess it's just what you get used to," he admitted with a wry smile.

As soon as they entered the outer lobby of the magazine offices, they were greeted by a shapely blonde who immediately made a fuss over Brad when she found out who he was. Ashley stifled a smile as the young woman's long painted fingers lingered on his chest as she pinned the name tag to his jacket lapel.

As they wandered around the display room, Brad was obviously uncomfortable with being a celebrity as several people in the crowd came up to talk with him.

The quality of the entries was undeniable. The competition had been stiff, but there was realism about Brad's photographs that made most of the others seem staged. A huge blue ribbon identified his entry, Picture Tour of Greystone Island, as the winner.

When the presentations had been made and Brad had received the winner's check, the generous gathering stood up and clapped. He was obviously surprised and appeared a little embarrassed that his hobby had merited such recognition. Several of the magazine's staff complimented him personally afterward.

As they took a taxi back to her apartment, he was strangely quiet as he held her hand. There had been no question about where he would spend the night.

When they walked into her large, beautifully decorated apartment, he gave a low whistle. "So this is your home sweet home."

"It is now…with you here," she said quietly "This morning, it was just lonely housing and that's all it will be when you leave."

"Are you sure?" he asked, searching her eyes for the truth. "What if I told you I might stay?"

"Here? In San Francisco?"

"I didn't want to say anything until I knew whether or not the feelings between us were still the same. The truth is, the magazine offered me a position of staff photographer. It would be similar to what I've been doing for Dora Hunskut. Taking photographs to illustrate magazine articles."

"And...and you're considering it?" she asked in amazement.

"These last few months have been nothing but empty drudgery. I'm more than ready for a change. I wouldn't mind traveling. Of course, I'd want to spend some time on the island during the summer and make sure Bill is taking care of Rusty. The chance to photograph a variety of places with natural beauty appeals to me. If you want to know the truth, I can't imagine getting paid what they've offered to do something I'd do for free."

She had a hard time believing her ears weren't deceiving her. "That sounds wonderful."

"I haven't told them I'd accept the offer. I wanted to see how things were with us first."

"And how are they?" she asked quietly.

"I guess it all depends on your answer." He put his hands lightly on her shoulders and looked into her eyes. "Will you marry me?"

She simply nodded because the sudden joy was too much for words. As his hands traced the yielding softness of her body, she leaned into his kiss with unleashed passion and desire.

When the telephone rang, she didn't make any move to answer it until the answering machine came on and she heard Lorrie's voice.

"Hi, Sis, are you there?"

Reluctantly Ashley pulled away from his embrace

and answered it. Her voice was husky as she said, "Yes, I'm here."

"Sorry to call you so late but I had to tell you that Michael and I are coming for Christmas after all. We talked it over and decided you shouldn't be alone."

"That sounds wonderful, Sis. How would you like to go to a Christmas wedding?"

"Whose?"

Ashley smiled and winked at Brad. "Guess."

* * * * *

A special treat for you from Harlequin Blaze!

Turn the page for a sneak preview of
DECADENT
by
New York Times *bestselling author*
Suzanne Forster

Available November 2006,
wherever series books are sold.

Harlequin Blaze—Your ultimate
destination for red-hot reads.
With six titles every month, you'll never guess
what you'll discover under the covers...

RUN, ALLY! Don't be fooled by him. He's evil. Don't let him touch you!

But as the forbidding figure came through the mists toward her, Ally kncw she couldn't run. His features burned with dark malevolence, and his physical domination of everything around him seemed to hold her like a net.

She'd heard the tales. She knew all about the Wolverton legend and the ghost that haunted The Willows, an elegant old mansion lost by Micha Wolverton nearly a hundred years ago. According to folklore, the estate was stolen from the Wolvertons, and Micha was killed, trying to reclaim it. His dying vow was to be reunited with the spirit of his beloved wife, who'd taken her life for reasons no one would speak of, except in whispers. But Ally had never put much stock in the fantasy. She didn't believe in ghosts.

Until now—

She still didn't understand what was happening. The

figure had materialized out of the mist that lay thick on the damp cemetery soil. A cool breeze and silvery moonlight had played against the ancient stone of the crypts surrounding her, until they joined the mist, causing his body to thicken and solidify right before her eyes. That was when she realized she'd seen this man before. Or thought she had, at least.

His face was familiar. . . so familiar, yet she couldn't put it together. Not with him looming so near. She stepped back as he approached.

"Don't be afraid," he said. His voice wasn't what she expected. It didn't sound as if it were coming from beyond the grave. It was deep and sensual. Commanding.

"Who are you?" she managed.

"You should know. You summoned me."

"No, I didn't." She had no idea what he was talking about. Two minutes ago, she'd been crouching behind a moss-covered crypt, spying on the mansion that had once been The Willows, but was now Club Casablanca. And then this—

If he was Micha, he might be angry that she was trespassing on his property. "I'll go," she said. "I won't come back. I promise."

"You're not going anywhere."

Words snagged in her throat. "Wh-why not? What do you want?"

"If I wanted something, Ally, I'd take it. This is about need."

His words resonated as he moved within inches of

her. She tried to back away, but her feet were useless. "And you need something from me?"

"Good guess." His tone burned with irony. "I need lips, soft and surrendered, a body limp with desire."

"My lips, my bod—?"

"Only yours."

"Why? Why me?" This couldn't be Micha. He didn't want any woman but Rose. He'd died trying to get back to her.

"Because you want that, too," he said.

Wanted what? A ghost of her own? She'd always found the legend impossibly romantic, but how could he have known that? How could he know anything about her? Besides, she'd sworn off inappropriate men, and what could be more inappropriate than a ghost? She shook her head again, still not willing to admit the truth. But her heart wouldn't play along. It clattered inside her chest. The mere thought of his kiss, his touch, terrified her. This wildness, it was fear, wasn't it?

When his fingertips touched her cheek, she flinched, expecting his flesh to be cold, lifeless. It was anything but that. His skin was smooth and hot, gentle, yet demanding. And while his dark brown eyes were filled with mystery and wonder, there was a sensitivity about them that threatened to disarm her if she looked too deeply.

"These lips are mine," he said, as if stating a universal fact that she was helpless to avoid. In truth, it was just that. She couldn't stop him.

And she didn't want to.

Find out how the story unfolds in…
DECADENT
by New York Times *bestselling author*
Suzanne Forster.
On sale November 2006.

Harlequin Blaze—Your ultimate
destination for red-hot reads.
With six titles every month, you'll never guess
what you'll discover under the covers…

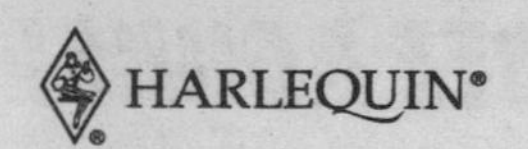

INTRIGUE

COMING NEXT MONTH

#951 A COLBY CHRISTMAS by Debra Webb
Colby Agency
It's Christmas Eve and everyone has gone home except agent Brad Gibson and receptionist Elaine Younger. By morning, would Christmas come for the Colby Agency?

#952 CRITICAL EXPOSURE by Ann Voss Peterson
Security Breach
Rand McClellan, a man who doesn't trust his own emotions, must help single-mother Echo Sloane, who stirs them up, take down a kidnapper with the uncanny power to manipulate them both.

#953 KEEPING CHRISTMAS by B.J. Daniels
Montana Mystique
When Chance Walker is hired to escort beautiful, stubborn Dixie Bonner back to Texas by Christmas, he uncovers some startling family secrets.

#954 DOUBLE LIFE by Amanda Stevens
He's a Mystery
When Ash Corbett returns to Jacob's Pass, Texas, just in time for a string of bodies to wash ashore, will former love Emma Novick recognize the man he's become?

#955 MAVERICK CHRISTMAS by Joanna Wayne
A mother fleeing with her children from killers. A sheriff learning to raise boys of his own. There's a reckoning and a Christmas miracle to be had in Montana.

#956 TO THE RESCUE by Jean Barrett
Trapped inside a remote castle, P.I. Leo McKenzie and Jennifer Rowan form an uneasy alliance to unmask a killer amongst the refugees seeking shelter from a relentless storm.

www.eHarlequin.com

HICNM1006